E. S. Carter

The Life and Adventures of E.S. Carter

Including a Trip Across the Plains and Mountains in 1852, Indian Wars in the Early

Days of Oregon in the years of 1854-5-6

E. S. Carter

The Life and Adventures of E.S. Carter
Including a Trip Across the Plains and Mountains in 1852, Indian Wars in the Early Days of Oregon in the years of 1854-5-6

ISBN/EAN: 9783337143763

Printed in Europe, USA, Canada, Australia, Japan

Cover: Foto ©Andreas Hilbeck / pixelio.de

More available books at **www.hansebooks.com**

The Life and Adventures

OF

E. S. CARTER

Including a Trip Across the Plains and Mountains in 1852,
Indian Wars in the Early Days of Oregon in
the Years of 1854-5-6.

--

Life and Experience in the Gold Fields of California, and
Five Years' Travel in New Mexico.

By E. S. CARTER, Maysville, Mo.

DEDICATED.

This book is dedicated to Mr. and Mrs. Enos Bray, as the author's appreciation for many kindnesses shown me in their home.　　　　E. S. C.

PREFACE.

This simple story of a plain man's experience in the west, is given to the public in the belief that the events narrated will be of interest to the many friends of the writer, and also prove that truthfulness of that saying, "that truth is more strange than fiction." The style is simple and straightforward, tending an interest as well as a charm to the narration. Some of the events are as thrilling as the most sensational novel. Yet many of my old friends in the states of Oregon and California can testify to the truthfulness of this narration.

E. S. CARTER, *Author*.

Maysville, Mo.

CONTENTS OF THE BOOK.

CHAPTER I.

I was born in Henry County, Indiana, September the 15th, 1836.

In 1843, father moved from there to Marion County and settled on Little Eagle Creek, about ten miles northwest of Indianapolis. There I spent the earliest days that I can remember. I was sitting in the shade of that old beechtree that stood at the foot of the hill, with my little dark-eyed companion by my side.

How happily the hours passed away! Time rolled on and my little friend took sick. She lay in her little bed two weeks, then bade us all good-bye and passed over the dark river. That was a sad blow to me, for I had lost the best friend of my childhood.

In the fall of 1850, father rented his farm, intending to visit my brothers, who lived in Platte County, Missouri. He soon had the team and wagon ready, and one bright morning in September, father, mother, brother and I started on our long road to Missouri.

Nothing of interest transpired that I can remember, until one evening, just before we reached a little stream in Illinois, we saw a gang of wild turkeys fly up from the side of the road and alight in a little grove about two hundred yards from the creek, where we camped for the night.

The next morning before daylight I took my gun, and my brother and I started for the grove where we had seen the turkeys alight the evening before. When we reached the grove we stopped under a big tree and waited for daylight so we could see where the turkeys were sitting. While looking up into the tree under which we were standing, we saw something on a limb about fifty feet above our heads, but it was not light enough to see what it was. I thought it might be a turkey. It was almost directly over our heads. I shot and it fell within six feet of where we stood.

To our surprise, it was a big fat turkey. A prouder boy never stood with a gun in his hand than I was while looking at the turkey lying at my feet.

After daylight I shot several times at the turkeys in the trees, and each time I shot the feathers flew, but they always carried off the bird. At last I got tired and gave it up, and we started back to our camp with our turkey. We sat doown to rest awhile under a big oak tree, where the ground was covered with acorns. I laid my gun on the ground and sat down with my back against the tree. The g..n was lying on the ground to my left. After we had rested awhile I turned over on my left side and reached for my gun. I could just reach the muzzle of it. Taking hold of the muzzle I pulled it towards me, when it went off. I jumped to my feet for I thought the bullet had gone through my body. While I was feeling of my legs to see if the bullet had gone through them, I looked down and saw spots of blood on my shirt bosom. Then I saw I had lost one joint of one of my fingers of my right hand. When we got to camp mother saw the blood on my hand and wanted to know what the matter was. I told her what had happened, but said: "That is nothing, see the fine turkey I have killed."

In due time we reached my brother's house in Platte County, about six miles south of Platte City. I had a nice time visiting my brothers' that winter, but in the spring my brothers got at my father to sell his farm in Indiana, and live in Missouri with them. It was mid-summer when I heard the sad news. I thought my heart would break for I wanted to go back to our dear old home again. The thought of leaving the dear old place where I had spent so many happy days was a sad thought to me. With tears in my eyes, I went to my father and told him how I longed to go back to the old place, and begged him not to sell. I told him if he sold his farm and let my brothers have the money I would go to Oregon in the spring, if I could get a chance.

In the fall of 1851 he sold out, and early in the spring of 1852 I got acquainted with Zura Duncan and his brother. They were fixing to start to Oregon as soon as spring opened up and the grass began to grow. I coaxed Mr. Duncan to let me go with him. Riley Duncan wanted a boy, so my baby brother went with him.

They had everything ready to start the 18th of April. About two weeks before we started I went down to where my father and mother were living with one of my brothers to bid them goodbye. When I told them I was going tears came into their eyes and they begged me not to go. I told them I was going, and had come to say a long farewell. They followed me to the gate and when I turned around and took them by their hands my eyes were full of tears. I kissed them, sobbed good-bye and turned and walked away. Little did I think that I had looked on their loving faces for the last time. Oh, if I had laid them in their silent graves, I could not have felt worse than I did when I left them at the gate crying to God to protect me while traveling to that far-off land. I had never been away from home two weeks before, but I knew it would be years before I would see them again. That bright morning in April I had looked on their loving faces for the last time unless I see them beyond the dark river of Death, which I intend to do with the help of Him who does all things well.

CHAPTER II.

On the 18th of April, we left Mr. Duncan's place, which is about three miles north of Camden Point, and on the 20th of April, we crossed the Missouri river on a flat-boat. We could take but one wagon at a time on the boat. There were twelve wagons in our company, each wagon drawn by from three to four yoke of oxen. In addition to those we had about seventy-five head of loose cattle.

When we got all our things across the river, we hitched up our teams and drove about three miles from the Fort, and encamped for the night on a little stream. Several of our old friends and neighbors who had helped us across the river, came and camped with us over night. The next morning, after we had hitched up, they shook hands with us and bade us God speed while on our journey across the plains.

After we left the little creek, we saw no more signs of civilization till we reached Fort Kearney, on Platte river.

The next place of any note that I can remember was Ash Hollow, on the Platte river, where Gen. Kearney killed so many Indians a few years before, and here we camped for the night.

The next night we camped on the river, and to our
left about two hundred yards was a little grove of ash
trees, where, about two weeks before, the Indians tied a
young man about seventeen years of age to one of the
trees and skinned him alive. He belonged to a family
that came from Illinois and was going to California. The
boy had sworn that he would kill the first Indian he saw,
and just before they camped for the night he saw an old
squaw sitting by the side of the road, and took his gun
out of the wagon and shot her dead. They had not been
camped more than half an hour when about two hundred
Sioux warriors came riding up the river towards the camp,
and seeing the old squaw lying beside the road, they
stopped four or five minutes and then galloped up to the
camp. There were eight wagons in the train. As soon
as the Indians came up they asked who had killed the
squaw, but no one would tell. At last the Indians told
them if they did not tell who had shot her they would
massacre the whole train. Then the captain pointed out
the boy who had shot the squaw. As soon as he was
pointed out the chief ordered two of the warriors to take
the boy. The boy ran and jumped into the wagon where
his mother and sister were sitting, and calling for his
father to save him, crawled under the blankets. The
Indians jumped into the wagon and pulled him out by
the heels, while his mother and sister cried as if their
hearts were breaking. They took him to that little grove
and treated him as already described in sight of the whole
camp. The wild screams of the boy as they tore the
skin from his body was more than his mother could stand

and she fainted. There was not an eye in the camp but what was filled with tears as those people listened to the wild despairing cries of the poor boy. It lasted about half an hour, then all was still and his friends went to the spot and cut him loose from the tree and buried him at the end of the little grove. A sad ending to a young life.

Not a day passed, after we left Ash Hollow, but we saw from one to five graves along the side of the road as we traveled up the Platte, river.

I well remember the night we camped opposite the Chimney Rock. It was standing at the foot of the hills about five miles south of the old emigrant road. That evening two young men drove up within a hundred yards of our camp and stopped for the night. I went over to their camp. One of the men was sick and died that night. I learned that there were four of them that had bought the team together and had started across the plains. Two of them had died before they reached this place. The next morning the young man buried his dead friend and with a sad heart he started back home. What became of him I do not know.

We crossed the North Platte near a craggy point of the hills, about two miles below Fort Laramie. After crossing over the hills we came to Sweet Water, a little stream where thousands of men, women and children that had started for the gold fields of California and Oregon have been laid to rest. For weeks and weeks we traveled up that little stream before we reached the foot of the Rocky Mountains.

Near the foot of the mountains we came to where a man kept a small trading post. Mr. Duncan bought a small brindle cow of him which we drove along with the train for several days. At last she got sullen and lay down and the only way we could get her up was to get off our horses and get in front of her; then she would jump up and take after us. As soon as we would get on our horses she would stop and then we could drive her several miles before she would lie down again. She kept this up for several days. One day one of the boys and I were driving her along behind the train. We were ascending a long hill and had nearly reached the summit when she laid down. Looking back I saw two men coming up the hill on foot, and further back was a wagon drawn by four yokes of oxen. The men soon overtook us and said: "Is your cow sick?" "No," said I, "she is only tired. Will you please kick her in the head and make her get up." One of the men stepped around in front of her and raised his foot. When she saw him raise his foot she jumped up and ran after him. He made for the wagon which was about one hundred yards away, and the race which followed was one of the most exciting I ever witnessed. The cow was about three feet behind when the man jumped into the wagon. A woman was sitting in the front end of the wagon. She laughed heartily when the man jumped into it. At last he raised his head above the wagon box and commenced to "te he" and we all roared with laughter. "Look yonder," said he, pointing off to one side of the road, "I think he is as badly frightened as I was, for he is still running." That night Mr. Duncan had the cow shot. He was afraid she might hurt some one.

We hardly knew when we reached the top of the mountains, for it seemed to me to be almost as level as the plains we had crossed. For miles and miles no elevations were visible except a few little hills. But in several places at the head of some little gulch we saw great piles of snow with wild flowers blooming not three feet away.

We got across the Rockies all right and went down on Bear river and camped one night at Soda Springs.

After we had crossed the mountains and got down into the valley we left the California road and started in a northerly direction towards Fort Hall on Snake river. There were but few soldiers at the Fort when we got there. We staid there one day and then traveled down the river till we reached Louis Fork of Bear-river. Here we forded the river which was swollen by the melting snow from the mountains until we had to block the beds of our wagons up almost to the top of the standards to keep our things from getting wet. There was a man in the train who had the tallest yoke of oxen I ever saw, and they were broke to ride same as a horse.

We camped there all night, and, in the morning we had everything ready for crossing the river. I got on one of the tall oxen which were hitched in the lead of a wagon. There was about thirty feet in the middle of the stream that swam all of the oxen except the one I was riding. The stream was about forty yards wide, and on the opposite side was a flat bottom covered with water. So many teams had crossed that it was quite muddy, and in places a man had to be careful not to turn his wagon over in the mud and water, which was between two and three feet deep.

I would take one team across and then go back for another. I had taken three or four teams across, and had gone back after another. The wagon contained an old man, his wife and two daughters, one about sixteen and the other about twelve years of age. We crossed the river all right, but, in making a turn around a bunch of willows the wagon started to turn over. I called to the old man to stop, and, jumping off the ox I was riding I ran to the wagon and caught hold of the bed. The old man got out and we tried to raise the wagon up, but could not do it, so we waited until some men came to help us. The girl was afraid the wagon would turn over, and she was determined to get out. She said she could walk through the mud to the shore. So I took her by the hands, and she jumped out into the mud up to her knees. I tried to lead her through the mud and water, but it was so thick that after going about twenty steps she stopped and said she could go no farther. I told her if she would get on my back I would carry her to dry land, about fifty yards away. "You can't carry me," she said: "Yes, I can easily carry you across," said I. But I had not calculated the amount of mud sticking to her dress, nor the depth of the mud and water through which I must wade.

I stooped over, and told her to climb on my back, after much coaxing, she attempted to do so; but in doing so she almost pushed me headforemost into the mud. I told her to put her arms around my neck and she could draw herself up out of the mud. She locked her arms around my neck and was soon on my back. Then I put my hands behind me, and around her and started for the shore with the mud and water running down my back. But I paid no attention to that, but pulled straight to the shore, amidst the yells and laughter of the men, women and children that were standing on either bank of the river looking at us. I thought they would hurt themselves laughing at me, while I was doing my best to get the poor girl to dry land.

Just as I reached the bank I struck my foot against a rock and fell, but landed the girl safely on dry ground. She took hold of my hand and tried to raise me up, and said: "Are you hurt? As soon as I could get my breath, I said: "No, only out of breath. You squeezed me so tight I could hardly breathe."

She looked into my face with tears in her eyes, and said: "You must excuse me, sir, I am not used to hugging boys." Then she laughed at me. I started back to help the other teams across, and by the middle of the afternoon we had all crossed over, and raised our tents, and the women commenced to cook supper. After supper was over, and the sun had gone down behind the western mountains we spread our blankets on the ground and lay down on them, and were soon fast asleep. Next morning we were up bright and early, and soon started on the road down the river.

We had been traveling a week down the river, when we came to a small stream that flowed down from the mountains, and emptied its waters into Snake river about three hundred yards below where we crossed. We arrived there about four o'clock, p. m., and went into camp, af.er picketing our horses and putting up our tents. I took a fish hook and went down to the river to fish. There were six or eight wigwams standing near the bank of the river. I went down close to the wigwams, and sat down on the bank, and threw my hook into the water. An old Indian came and stood by me for some time, then he took hold of my pole and drew my hook out of the water, took the lead off the line and threw it into the river, and shook his head at me, then threw the hook back into the water with a grunt, as much as to say: "All right."

The little Indian boys came and sat down all around me and would laugh heartily when I caught a fish. It was almost dark when I started back to camp, taking with me quite a mess of fish that I had caught.

Two days after we left there a company of emigrants camped at the same place and the Indians stole all their horses and cattle and drove them off into the mountains. Whether the emigrants ever got any of them back I never heard.

In due time we reached the foot of the Cascade mountains and the night we camped there I took the mountain fever and was hauled across the mountains in a wagon. We crossed the mountains right at the foot of Mount Hood, which is 11,225 feet above the sea level.

It took us about three days and it was the roughest road I ever traveled. The teams had to go almost straight up and down to get across the deep gulches and canons. We reached the Willamette valley, twelve miles south of Oregon city near a little stream called Pudding creek. I had a cousin living there, who took me to his house and sent to Oregon City for a doctor. I lay there six weeks before I was able to get out of bed. I often thought while lying there with the fever burning my brow if my mother were only here by my side with her loving hand on my brow, I would soon be well again. For a lonely boy in a foreign land, sick and among strangers, there is nothing so dear to him as a mother's love, and although she be far away, the thought of home and mother is always dear to him.

It was near the middle of September when we landed in Oregon. When I got able to get around it was late in the fall.

That winter I got acquainted with a young man by the name of Charley Williams. He had come to Oregon in the fall of 1849 and was in the Kiyous war in Eastern Oregon in 1850.

During the winter of 1852 and spring of 1853 there was quite an excitement about the gold that had been found on the North and South Santiam rivers. During the summer Charley and I each bought a pony and started up the South Santiam to prospect near the foot of the mountains.

CHAPTER III.

We were prospecting near the head of a little stream that flows out of the Cascade mountains, near the foot of Mt. Jefferson. My partner and I had been working hard for three or four days, without finding enough gold to pay. We had erected a rude shelter, where we did our cooking and sleeping. On our way to our cabin on the evening of the fourth day, we met an Indian. He was on his way to the burnt district on the south of the Santiam, to gather berries. He seemed surprised to see us there in that lonely place, but asked no questions.

There were about one thousand acres in that district that was densely covered with dew-berries. Passing down the mountain side, he was soon lost to our view.

After we had eaten our supper, and were sitting down smoking our pipes, I told my partner I did not like the looks of the Indian. We had seen no sign of Indians up to the moment we saw him standing before us. I thought they had seen us before and had sent him out as a spy, and that he had made the excuse that he was going after berries.

Before this, we had been up the mountain quite a distance, and had found where there had been a volcano, the lava covering the ground for some distance. By traveling over the lava bed we found where the burnt rock looked like honeycomb, making a hole large enough for a man to crawl in and hide from the observation of anyone that was passing. It was not more than half a mile away and we decided to pick up our blankets and grub and go examine the place and if we found it a good place to hide in would leave our things there and return and watch our old camp and see if there were any Indians prowling around. We had some candles we had brought up from the valley. We found the place without much difficulty. My partner crawled in first and I handed him our blankets and guns, then I crawled in after him. We had gone but a short distance when I told my partner to light a candle, as there could be no danger of being seen as we were already ten feet in the cave; but imagine our surprise when the rays of our light shone forth upon the form of a beautiful woman on a bed of leaves, bound hand and foot. We stood like men who had been struck dumb with horror, gazing on the face of that lone woman. A light sound came from the bed of leaves which called us back to our senses. I stepped up to the side of the woman and laid my hand gently on her forehead. We had thought her dead but *thank God!* she still lived. She had fainted and was yet unconscious. We found her bound, her hands behind her back and her feet close together.

While coming up the mountain side we had noticed a basin of water and my partner took our canteen and returned soon with some fresh water. We bathed her face and rubbed her hands for a few minutes before we could discover any sign of life. Finally she slowly opened her eyes and looked around, and seeing us standing there she cried with a wild despairing cry: "Kill me, kill me, and put me out of my misery."

We urged her to be calm, assuring her we were friends. I had cut the cord that bound he hands and feet, so she could sit up. She raised up, looked around and asked: "Where am I." I gave her some water to drink, and told her where she was, and how we came to find her. She told us how she came there.

She said: "My father lived about thirty miles from Eugene City, Oregon, in the Willamette valley. I had often heard of the burnt district, famous for its berries, and my brother and I had gone to the patch three days before, and the next day when we got up our team was gone. Brother had gone in search of the horses. I got breakfast and waited for him to come back; but as he did not return, I went to canning up the berries we had gathered the day before. I was busy at my work when I heard a noise behind me. I thought it was my brother and when I turned round, right in front of me stood a big dirty looking Indian. "Ugh, white squaw work, good squaw, Indian love squaw."

I was frightened and hallowed. He jumped and gathered me. That was the last I knew until we were more than half way up the mountain. He had stopped to rest when I came to. I begged him to let me go back and tried to get away, but he threw me down on the ground and tied a stick in my mouth, then tried to make me walk, but I would not so he carried me up the mountain and put me in this hole and bound my hands and feet and left, saying he would be back in one sun and take me to his wigwam on the other side of the mountain."

I asked her how long she had been here. She did not think she had been here more than four or five hours. I then gave her some bread and meat and told her to eat some as it would require all her strength and courage, for I knew from what the Indian had told her he would return for her.

I told my partner I thought he had gone for other Indians to help him carry her over the mountain. We had two canteens so we went to the basin and filled them with water. We thought of leaving at once, but we did not know soon he would be back, and if we were to start and they were to overtake us in the mountains, we would be in more danger than we would be in here, for we would be on the lookout, and they would not catch us napping.

We were well armed and had plenty of ammunition. My partner was brave as a lion. He said he was good for four or five Indians. He was an old Indian fighter. He had been in many a scramble with them. By the time we got everything ready it was getting dark. It was a close evening, and the stars shone brightly. A man from our hiding place could see quite a distance, so we waited and watched. I don't think we had been there more than two hours, when we heard a light noise. "What is it?" I asked. All was quiet for a few minutes,

3

then we heard the sound again. It was coming. I thought it was an Indian, but my partner thought it was some wild animal. The sound was getting closer every minute.

It soon came in sight. It was a large bear, one of the most dangerous animals a man has to contend with in the mountains. By this time it was within forty yards. I raised my gun to shoot, but my partner cried: "Hold, you fool, one shot might be our death warrant." He came within a short distance of our retreat, then reared up on his hind legs, sniffed the air, then turned and slowly started back. Then all was quiet again. Just as the bear had left Miss Prine came up to where we were sitting and said: "Dear friends, I was so lonely in there that I must speak or die of loneliness." "Speak low, Miss Prine," said I, "for the Indians may be in hearing of the smallest sound." "Give me a pistol so I can help defend my own life." "Bravo!" cried my partner, handing her a revolver. I asked her if she knew how to use one. She laughed and said: "Yes, I have been used to handling a gun and pistol ever since I was a little girl." "And you are not afraid to use it if it becomes necessary?" She said with a frown: "I would rather blow my own brains out than be again in the Indian's clutches." I tried hard to get her to go back and take a rest, but no, she would rather stay there and see the Indians coming. What a brave woman she was. Her eyes sparkled with true grit of a noble woman. How proud she stood there bidding defiance to the storm that must soon come. We were confident in the position we were in we could hold them off for awhile, but could not hold out long for we only had two canteens of water and a small amount of grub, and we did not know how the Indians might come.   So we were very uneasy, and the night dragged heavily along.   We never slacked our vigil for one moment.   It was somewhere near four o'clock when we heard a light noise way down the mountain.   I said: "Miss Prine, they are coming."   "Well, let them come; we are ready to welcome them with powder and lead, and they will find me no weak woman when I have a pistol to defend myself with."   My partner gathered hold of her hand said: "Those are my sentiments, too; we will stop the redskins from coming or all die together." As they came nearer the noise grew louder.   They did not take their usual caution for they thought they were coming to torment a defenseless woman.

CHAPTER IV.

How sadly they were disappointed. It seemed to me it had been hours since we heard the first sound of them coming. We were anxious to see how many there were of them. At last we could hear them talking. "Listen," said Miss Prine, "there is a white man with them; I can tell by the sound of his voice." They were talking a jargon. The Indian has a peculiar grunt when talking, while the white man has not. They stopped about one hundred yards below where we were, and I heard the white man say: "How much farther is it to the place?"

Miss Prine said she thought she knew the voice. "If I am correct, it is one of the worst young men that ever lived in the Williamette valley." When they had come a little closer, we could see there were six, five Indians and a white man.

My partner said: Don't shoot until I give the word." Miss Prine was standing close to my side. Not a muscle moved. She looked in the starlight like a statue, only her eyes were blazing for revenge. By the time they had come in fifty yards of us the word was given. "Take good aim and fire." At the sound of the rifles, two Indians fell. The sounds of the two rifles were so close together that it was almost impossible to tell that there had been but one shot fired. We dropped down and reloaded as quick as possible, while Miss Prine watched the Indians with her pistol in hand.

The Indians seemed to be thunderstruck. The white man was cursing the Indians, telling them to come on, there was only one man there and they could soon overpower him, then he would give them the reward he had promised. Not only that, but he would let them have the white man to torture.

While the conversation was going on, Miss Prine raised too high above the rocks. It seemed they all saw her at once, and made a rush to capture her, just as we had finished loading and were ready to receive them. The Indians fired just as we raised up. One ball struck the lock of my partner's gun and broke it. My ball caused another savage to bite the dust. The white man sprang toward my partner with his pistol drawn, and would have killed him had not Miss Prine shot him in the breast. It would have done you good to have seen the two Indians who were unhurt run down the mountain. I went to see if the white man was dead, and found that he had only fainted from loss of blood. My partner brought the canteen of water. As soon as Miss Prine looked in his face, she said it was Joe Brown, the California outlaw.

We bathed his face in cold water and he soon revived. We had stopped the blood. I raised his head and laid it on my lap. He opened his eyes and with a wild stare he looked at Miss Prine and said: "Mary Prine I have lost my revenge and you have killed me. I do not blame you for shooting me, for if I had gotten you in my power inside the prison walls would have been a paradise to the life you would have led with me. Give me water, I am dying with thirst." We gave him some water and after waiting quite awhile he resumed: "Mary, I hired the Indian to bring you here"—and he fell over, dead. I asked Mary (as we shall hereafter call her) if she knew this man. She said: "He had come into our neighborhood about three years ago and hired to a near neighbor. I had seen him several times while working there but never had an introduction until one night at a social party given at Mr. Berry's house. I danced two or three times with him and incurred his ill will by not accepting his company home. He vowed vengeance, telling me I would be sorry for this some time. He shortly left the neighborhood and no one ever knew what became of him."

In a shallow hole we buried him, without one tear of sympathy and left him there in the hands of his offended God.

By this time day had broken and the stars were fast disappearing. It was time we had come to some conclusion what to do. We knew it would be hazardous for us to go back down the valley, for it was thirty. miles to the nearest settlement and there were a great many Indians living along the Santiam river, and that the Indians would soon be on our track. Mary said she had an uncle living on the east side of the mountains on a little creek called Ochasco. She said he was an old mountaineer and had been living there for several years trapping. She thought if we could reach there we would be safe.

It was between forty and fifty miles to his place. After being assured by Mary that she could make the trip on foot, we made a hasty start knowing the Indians would soon be on our trail. The burnt rock thrown up by the volcano, was a great hindrance to trailing us, and thus protected we made the start for the other side of the mountain to find her uncle. We filled our canteens with water and left the place where a few hours before we were contending for our lives. We started in a southeasterly direction along the mountain. We were careful not to displace any of the rocks, so the Indians could find our trail. We made a successful day's journey without seeing any sign of Indians. Often when we were near a high point, one would go up and look back to see if any Indians were in sight. Being tired and hungry, we were casting about for a safe retreat for the night, when we discovered a large rock under which we could crawl out of sight, and be sheltered from the cool mountain air. Under that rock we ate bread and dried venison, fearing to build a fire, lest our whereabouts might be discovered. We were talking of our late experience, when Mary broke out crying, saying: "Oh, what will my poor mother think when they find I am lost?"

We took our blankets and made Miss Prine as comfortable a place to sleep as it was possible to do under the circumstances, and then we talked for some time about the cruelty of Indians and the uncertainty of life traveling through this wild mountain country, when we were liable to meet straggling bands of them any hour of the day.

I advised Mary to lie down and take some rest, for I knew she must be tired, for our long journey up the mountain was very tiresome, as many times we would have to get down and crawl round craggy points of rocks as one misstep would precipitate us over the bluffs to alight on rocks a thousand feet below. 1 told her my partner and I would take turn about watching, so we would not be taken by surprise. She laid down and was soon in the land of dreams, living over the happy hours of childhood.

After she had laid down we lighted our pipes and sat talking over the incidents of the day until a late hour, when all at once there was one of the wildest piercing yells I ever heard in all my life. It came from over our heads and we supposed it was on the rock we were under. We were ready in a moment with our guns to defend ourselves. Mary awoke, asked what was the matter. We told her it must be some wild animal that had tracked us to our retreat. We listened a long time but never heard anything more.

The night soon passed away and we took an early start on our journey up the mountains. . Between twelve and one o'clock we reached the summit and sat down to rest for we were all tired and hungry.

We had a little dried venison left, which we ate, and after resting awhile we started down the mountain. We kept a sharp lookout for deer. My partner said he was almost sure he would find one near some of the many gulches that were in sight away down the mountain. We had got about one-third of the way down, when, going around the head of the gulch, we saw a deer. My partner shot and killed it and we soon had it dressed. We looked around and found a place between two large rocks where we could build a small fire that could not be seen far off and we soon had some venison roasting. By the time we had finished eating the sun had sunk behind the mountain and it was getting dark. We found some sticks which we fixed against the rocks and spread our blankets over them so Mary could sleep without being exposed to the heavy dew that falls in the mountains that time of year. There was nothing that disturbed our hiding that night only the bark of coyotes and the howling of the mountain wolves.

Next morning after a hasty meal we started down the mountain in better spirits than we had been in since starting, for we had not seen an enemy, nor any sign of one.

We were approaching the foot of the mountain when a little to our left we saw a large hill that looked from one to two hundred feet high. The top was covered thick with wild, shaggy brush. I told my partner one of us had better go on top and reconnoitre, for from that point the valley could be seen for miles around.

He went to the top and Mary and I sat down to await his return. He had not been gone more than half an hour when he returned in a hurry, telling us that there was a large stream not more than two miles off, and that down the stream at a big bend he saw about thirty Indian wigwams, and that he saw four Indians not more than a mile away who were coming straight for the knoll. We picked

up and started in a southerly direction along the foothills.
We kept up a brisk step for about eight or ten miles, when
we stopped in a thick bunch of bushes not more than half
a mile from the river.

My partner said for me and Mary to stay here and he
would go and see if there was any chance to cross the
stream.   He was gone quite awhile and we were getting
very uneasy when we saw him coming.   He told us he
had seen where several bands of Indians had been traveling
up and down the river, and that about a mile up the river
he had found a drift where he thought we could make a
raft to cross the river on.   With a small hatchet we
trimmed the dry limbs from the logs and had them in the
stream tied together in about an hour.   We piled dry
limbs on the logs, then put our things on top and all got
on; then with long poles we pushed the raft across.   As
soon as we got our things on the bank we cut the strings
that held the logs together and let them float down
the stream.

We had just got our things back from the bank and
had set down to rest a little when we saw five or six
Indians about three quarters of a mile away following our
trail towards the drift where we made our raft.   Across the
valley two or three miles we could see a large craggy point
of rocks.   It looked like it was standing alone in the
middle of the valley.   We knew it would not do for them
to see us here, so we crawled back from the bank of the
river until we got to a bunch of small bushes; so we
worked our way from one bunch to another till we got to
the knoll.   By that time the sun was down.   When we got

there we found we could not climb to the top from that side so we had to go around quite a distance before we could find a place we could climb.

Before we got on top it was quite dark, but the stars shone brightly, so we could see if there was any place where we could make a stand with any show of success, if we were attacked.   To our great joy we found the rocks at one place piled up about eight feet above the rest of the knoll.   We piled up some rocks and soon had a snug place to defend ourselves in.   After we had got all our things up and examined our arms, we sat down to meditate on what the morrow might bring forth.

CHAPTER V.

We did not think they would find us tonight, but the thoughts of tomorrow made us feel sad indeed. If Mary had only been at home and we had been alone, we would have been comparatively happy, for we knew that if she was to fall into their hands death would be preferable. We fixed our blankets the best we could for Mary to lie on and take some needed rest after the fatigue and anxiety of the day. She fell asleep with her cheeks and brow exposed to the cold mountain air, but still she slept on. "May God protect her from the hands of the cruel enemies," was the silent prayer of the watchers. My partner watched till I took a short nap, then I awoke and got him to lie down awhile. Just at the break of day we saw smoke curling up through the tops of the trees in a little grove about a quarter of a mile away. We had been watching only a few minutes when we saw five Indians slip out from among the trees and commence looking around, as we supposed for our trail. Our surmises proved true, as they soon found our trail and started very cautiously along toward the knoll. Every few steps they stopped and looked in every direction. If they followed our trail they would have to come close to the foot of the bluff that we were on. My partner said when they get even with us he would make a little noise, enough to attract their attention, then we must take good aim and be sure not to miss. It was but a few minutes till the word was given and two Indians dropped to the ground, never to follow the trail of the white man again. The other three broke and ran. Mary fired her pistol and we fired two or three times, but whether any of them were hit we never knew.

We could see a strip of timber some five miles away and we supposed it was the creek her uncle lived on that they called Ochaco creek.

We packed our things and started toward that without even getting anything to eat. It took us but a short time to reach the timber and to our great joy we found a little stream, running in a northerly direction. We followed down the stream as fast as we could go for we were afraid that the Indians that we shot at might get reinforced and overtake us before we found Mary's uncle. We had gone down the stream three miles where we saw three or four horses feeding around the knoll about two hundred yards below. We dropped behind some bushes for we thought they were Indian ponies. My partner took his gun and crept towards them to see if there was any Indians around. Mary and I sat down and waited, we thought a long time for him to come, and begun to be very uneasy, but directly we saw him coming around the hill with his gun thrown over his shoulder and beckoning us to come. So we started to him in a hurry. He told us he had seen no Indians, but down below about half a mile he saw a cabin and smoke coming out of the chimney. So we started to the cabin to see if we could find out where Mr. Prine lived. I knocked at the door. A man came to it. I asked if he knew a man on the creek by the name of Prine? "Yes," he said, "that is my name." I asked him if he had a brother living in Oregon by the name of David. "Yes, I have a brother there by that name." Then I introduced Mary to him, and while he was glad to see her, said he was sorry she was here under the present circumstances.

He made us welcome to his cabin. After preparing us a good meal and we had satisfied our appetites, he wanted to know how we came to be there. We narrated to him how we happened to find Mary and all the incidents of our journey.

He then told us that a man from the Dells had told him that the Indians were on the warpath all over the country and were massacreing defenseless women and children, and he was running bullets when we knocked at the door, and that he was making preparation to go to the Dells, as he expected to be attacked here at any time. He said that three days ago he had seen about twenty Indians crossing the knoll, pointing across the creek. He said he had intended going there on horseback, but now there were four of us and he had but two ponies, we would walk. I asked how far it was and was told that it was one hundred and twenty miles. Mr. Prine was afraid Mary could not walk that distance, but Mary, laughing, told him he need have no fear for her, and so it was decided we would all walk together.

We baked a lot of bread to take with us. Mr. Prine had plenty of dried venison. We had it all packed and ready to start in a short time, but Mr. Prine said we had better not start until after sundown. The sun was about three hours high. He told us that we had better lie down and take a nap, as we had but little rest since the night we rescued Mary from the cave. So we were soon fast asleep. It did not seem to me that it had been twenty minutes when **Mr.** Prine awoke us and said it was time we were on the road.

He had supper ready for us and after eating we were soon on the road. He said he knew a path along the foothills and we had better take that for we wouldn't be half so likely to meet straggling bands of Indians as we would if we took the road down the valley.

Mr. Prine had been hunting and trapping in the mountains for a long time and was well acquainted with the customs of the Indians.

We traveled as fast as we could, but kept a sharp lookout. About the break of day we came to a craggy point of rocks that Mr. Prine said was the only place where we could hide with any safety for ten miles. We soon found a place where we would be safe from observation. Mr. Prine entertained us with the narrating of his many hair-breadth escapes in the mountains with wild beasts and Indians. He said with all the ups and downs through his checkered life he never felt as uneasy for anything as he did for that poor girl.

We took turn about watching while the others slept. About the middle of the afternoon we saw a band of ten or a dozen Indians coming down the valley. They were going toward a log cabin about a mile below. The anxiety we felt while watching them can never be told, for we knew if there were women and children their doom was sealed. We soon saw the house was on fire and knew by their standing around there was no one there. They soon left, going down the valley.

By this time the day was far spent. Mr. Prine had taken a canteen to a little creek and filled it with water. As soon as he got back we awoke Mary and all ate heartily of the cold grub. By the time we had finished eating the sun had set and we resumed our journey along the foothills without meeting with any accident or seeing an enemy. We traveled about twenty-five miles and camped in a thick bunch of bushes during the day. We saw several squads of Indians traveling up the valley.

The day was hot, and before noon we had drank all the water we had. Mr. Pfine knew where he could reach the creek within a mile and took a canteen and went after water. While on his way he had seen some Indians but had secreted himself behind some rocks until they had passed. After satisfying our thirst and eating a hearty meal of bread and dried venison, we were again ready to start.

Mr. Prine had an old friend living down the valley by the name of Springer and he thought we could reach his place by daylight. About four o'clock in the morning, after coming through a small patch of timber, we saw Mr. Springer's house about one hundred and fifty yards away. We stopped to see if we could hear anything. We did not know but they had gone to the Dells fcr safety. We had only stopped, when we were startled by a wild despairing cry like one in the agony of death, coming from the house. We broke and ran for the house. Just as we got in front of the house two Indians came out of the door bearing a young girl in their arms.

CHAPTER VI.

I struck one of the Indians with my gun. He let loose of her and jumped back, but not soon enough to escape the blow which brought him senseless to the ground. The other started to run and had made but a few steps when my partner shot him dead. Mr. Prine jumped into the house, for we heard a noise in there. He had just got inside when two Indians faced him with their deadly tomahawks in their hands. My partner rushed to the rescue and then ensued one of the most deadly combats I ever witnessed, which resulted in the spirits of two noble warriors taking their flight to the happy hunting ground. Miss Springer had fainted when the Indians gathered her and Miss Prine was trying to restore her while the fight was going on in the house. As soon as the Indians were dispatched we went into the other room and there on the floor was a sight that would chill the blood of the bravest man and fill his eyes with tears. There on the floor was Mrs. Springer lying with two of her little children by her side with their heads split wide open.

I heard Mary calling and went to see what she wanted. Miss Springer had partially come to. She told me to look after that Indian, as she thought she heard him moving. I examined him and found he was still alive but unconscious. He lived but a short time. I got Mary some water and she bathed the girl's face and hands. She was soon on her feet.

We took some cloths and bound around Mrs. Springer's and the children's heads and laid them side by side. I told Mary what we had done and for her to break the news to the poor girl as gently as she could, and after awhile to bring her to see them. When she came in and saw them she gave one wild scream and fell senseless to the floor. We did all in our power to bring her to. Through the kind and loving care of Mary she at last opened her eyes. That lonely child but a short time before had a loving mother, a sister and a brother, but now an orphan. We asked her where her father was. She said: "Day before yesterday he started for the Dells and told us he would be back last night, but did not come."

We made some rough boxes and dug a grave and put them in it, with sad hearts and weeping eyes. We covered them up to lie there until the resurrection morn.

We had not seen any Indians during the day, and the sun was sinking behind the western hills. Miss Springer went to the grave and in agony of her loneliness wept bitterly over the quiet sleepers, then bidding them a loving long farewell, she turned and left the mound. After she returned to the house we picked up and were soon on the road to the Dells. Nothing transpired that night worth mentioning. The girls were very tired when we camped by a stream about eighteen miles from the Dells.

Miss Springer's sorrow was great. She knew not what had become of her father. She believed the Indians had killed him. Her lamentations were sorrowful to hear. I told her I thought if they had come across him they might have taken him a prisoner and there was yet some hope. I told her as soon as we got to the Dells I would get a party of men and search for him. We will find his body if he is killed. If we find nothing of him we will know they have taken him prisoner. If he is a prisoner in their camp we will rescue him and bring him back if it is in the power of man to do it.

The next night we reached the Dells in safety. We found the town in great excitement. Men and women were coming in from all directions, telling startling tales about the Indians massacreing women and children and burning every house they came across. There was but one hotel in the town and we took the girls to it. I went and spoke to the landlord and asked him if he knew a man that lived between here and the Ochaco valley by the name of John Springer? "Yes, I know him well; he was here yesterday. I saw him start home; what about him?" Then I told him how we came to have the two girls with us, and the fight we had at Mr. Springer's house and how we found Mrs. Springer and the two children lying dead on the floor, and that we came up just in time to save his only child. Then I told him how we found Mary on the other side of the mountain, and all about our trip down the valley.

Mr. Swinney soon collected a few young men and was on the way to Mr. Springer's house to see if they could find any trace of him, and in two days they were back and said that beyond doubt they had taken him prisoner, for they seen a trail where a large band of Indians had crossed the road and were going in the direction of the Green mountain.

At the head of a little stream that plowed out of the mountain there was a fine spring; that often the Indians in the fall of the year camped there to hunt game and we believed they had Mr. Springer there a prisoner, and if not rescued soon, they would burn him at a stake.

That night a boat came up from Portland, Oregon, and was going back in the morning. I told Mary I would get her a ticket to Portland on the boat. She was very anxious to get home. I paid her fare on the boat and gave her money to pay expenses and get a seat in the stage that runs up the valley past her father's house. Everything was in readiness in the morning for Mary's departure. We went down with her to the boat and when we came to bid her goodbye there was not an eye but shed tears of sorrow at parting from one that had been with us through so many trials and difficulties in the last two weeks, but she was going home where she would be safe from the cruel Indians that surrounded her here. After bidding us all farewell she stepped aboard the boat. It was soon pushed off from the wharf and while it was floating down the stream Mary was standing on the deck waiving her handkerchief at us till it floated out of sight down the river.

CHAPTER VII.

I took Miss Springer back to the hotel. She was almost heart-broken at parting from Mary. As my partner and I started out for a walk I told him if we could find a man that was acquainted with the country we would try and get him to go with us and see what had become of Mr. Springer. We stopped at a grocery store to get some tobacco. There was quite a crowd of men in there listening to a man telling what a time he had in the Green mountains once while hunting. He was a broad shouldered, muscular man about thirty-five years of age, with long red hair and sandy whiskers. He went by the name of "Sandy." I soon had a chance to speak to him. I told him I wanted to talk to him privately on some important business. He took my arm and we started in a southeasterly direction and soon came to a small grove of willows that were growing on the bank of Snake river. Charley Williams, my partner, overtook us here. After seating ourselves I told him of the lonely girl at the hotel and of her father who was thought to be a captive in the hands of a band of Indians camped somewhere near the foot of Green mountains, where they say there is a large spring. "I thought from what you said in the store you were acquainted in that part of the country.   There are three of us going and we need you for a guide and assistant in rescuing that man.   Will you go?"   "I will."

We returned to town and found Mr. Prine, and after talking over our plans, decided to start the next night.

During the day the citizens commenced to raise volunteers and by evening of the next day they had a company of sixty-five men.   They had elected their officers and would be ready to start in a few days.   They were going up Umatilla valley.   They tried to get us to join their company but we refused and stuck to our own plan to go alone.   By sundown we were ready to start on our lonely journey.   I told Miss Springer we were going that night in search of her father.

That night we traveled up Snake river about eighteen miles and camped in a bend of the river where there were a lot of willows growing.

During the day we saw several bands of Indians going up the river on the other side from us about as fast as their ponies could carry them.   Late in the afternoon there were two Indians rode up to the river opposite to us and rode into the water and let their ponies drink. We thought they would discover us but they soon turned and rode out of the water and took up the valley and were soon out of sight.   Sandy told us he thought it was about twenty miles from here to Umatilla creek, and he thought we would reach it by traveling hard all night. It was too dangerous for us to travel by day, for if we were seen by the Indians it would be a miracle if any of us got back alive.

We reached the Umatilla valley about day break. We followed up the valley about a mile and found a tolerable safe place to hide during the day. There was nothing that disturbed us that day. While one stood guard the balance slept. So the day soon passed away and we were again ready for the night's journey.

We followed up the creek about four miles to the mouth of a little stream that came down from the mountains Sandy said that there was a safe retreat up this stream where we could hide in safety, about eight miles from there, and that he had stayed there many a night when out hunting. We reached the place long before daylight. It was a splendid place to defend ourselves against wild beasts and Indians if any should attack us. We kept a sharp lookout that day, for Sandy told us we were not more than five miles from the spring where we thought the Indians were camped. We saw no sign of them through the day—only an old Indian and a squaw late in the evening going in the direction of the spring. Sandy and Williams said they would go and see if there were any Indians camped there, and if possible, find out if Mr. Springer was a prisoner. As soon as it was dark they started. It was about twelve o'clock when they got back. They had taken a roundabout way to get to the camp. The Indians' wigwams were set as close to the mountains as they could get them. They had come around on the side of the mountain as close to their camp as it was safe. As soon as they found a safe place to hide where they would not be seen by Indians prowling near the camp, they sat down to watch and wait.   They had been there but a few minutes when there rode into camp two Indians.   There were thirty wigwams and not less than two hundred warriors in camp.

It was not long until they knew there was something unusual that had happened, for the warriors had collected in groups all over the camp and all seemed to be excited about something.   Sandy said he knew enough of their language if he could only get close to that wigwam, pointing to one that stood near the foot of the mountain, to find out what the excitement was about.   He crawled down as close as he could and lay flat on the ground to catch every word.   He had been lying down but a short time till he learned there were a company of soldiers camped down the Umatilla creek, and just before the break of day they intended to surprise the camp, and on their return would burn their white prisoners at the stake.

As soon as he learned what they intended to do he hurried back to where he left Mr. Williams, and then they come back to us fast as they could and told all they had learned.   Sandy said it would not do to let Indians surprise the soldiers.   We knew it must be the company from the Dells.   So Sandy started to put them on their guard.

In about two hours he reached the camp and told them what the Indians intended doing.   The captain called up his men and informed them of the danger they were in.   They were soon ready to meet them when they came.   About one mile from where they were camped there was a narrow gap through the hill that they thought the Indians must come through. So they went there and formed two lines; then waited for them to come. As soon as the Indians had got about half way through the gap the soldiers fired into them, taking the Indians so completely by surprise that they broke and ran, with the boys after them shooting as fast as they could load their guns.

As soon as Sandy left to warn the soldiers we started to the Indian camp, for we knew if they attacked the soldier's camp they would leave but few warriors behind. It took us but a short time to reach their camp. There were but few sitting around and soon all was quiet. There was a log hut standing about fifty yards from the foot of the mountain. We crawled close up to it and tapped lightly on the door, then waited a short time and tapped again. We heard a low voice inquiring: "Who is there?" We answered: "Friends." We then examined the door and found it fastened with a piece of iron driven into one of the logs. This we soon removed and on opening the door, found Mr. Springer in one corner with both feet and hands bound. We cut the cords and lifted him to his feet. It was some little time before he could stand alone. We soon reached the mountain without raising any alarm. We had only time to get far enough away to hide when we saw straggling Indians coming into camp. We knew when we saw them coming in that the boys had beaten them off.

We hurried back to our hiding place, knowing that Sandy would return there as soon as he could. He came back about twelve o'clock and told us of the fight and said the soldiers intended joining us here about nightfall and during the night to surprise the Indians in their camp.

After Mr. Springer had eaten a hearty meal he told us how the Indians had captured him and bound him to his pony and had taken him to their camp where we found him. We broke to him as gently as we could the sad news concerning his family. It was almost too much for him and we thought for a time he had lost his reason. We tried to console him by telling him of his only child alone in the Dells, waiting for him to come back to her. "My child, my child!" he cried, "I will live for you and to revenge the death of my poor wife and children!"

Just as the sun was sinking behind the western horizon the soldiers arrived at our camp, and after some consultation, it was decided not to attack until about three o'clock. Guards were stationed to keep watch while the others slept. At two o'clock we were up and as soon as we had finished our meal the boys were all formed in line and divided in two. The captain took command of one squad and Sandy was placed in command of the other. Mr. Springer, Prine and I went with Sandy's band. We were to go around on the mountain and come up on the back of their camp, while the company was to go up the valley. They were to give us plenty of time to get around close to the camp. Then we were to wait till we heard them fire. Then we were to pitch into them, and thus have them between two fires. We got to our position without being seen by the Indians. We had been there but a few moments when we heard the warwhoop given by the Indians in that wild piercing yell that only can be given by the Indian.

CHAPTER VIII.

The boys went after them and gave it to them as they ran. The Indians broke back toward the foot of the mountain. Then we opened fire on them; with a yell we rushed into their midst, using our guns for a club. It seemed to me that Mr. Springer had the strength of a giant; he was dealing death to every Indian that came in reach of him. It was but a short time before they broke and ran in all directions. •The boys killed several as they were climbing the mountain. We burned their wigwams and all other traps that we could find. By this time it was broad daylight, and the captain called us together. There were ten men who did not answer to the call. We commenced looking around to see what had become of them. We found two of them dead and eight wounded. Some with flesh wounds, one with a leg broken, and one with an arm. We dressed their wounds the best we could, then we dug one large grave, and laid two to rest in it, side by side. With sad hearts we covered them over and left them to sleep that sweet sleep that knows no waking. We took the wounded and went back to where we camped the day before. They all got along very well but the man with the broken leg. We had to fix a pony so he could lie down on him.

We camped here all day and night. In the morning early we were ready to start on our way back to the Dells. It would take us about three days to get back for we had to travel slowly on account of the wounded.

Sandy told the captain that he had better keep a sharp lookout for the Indians, for he believed they would attack us before two days. That night we camped on the Umatilla creek. We had seen no Indians during the day and that was a bad sign for us. Sandy said he was confident by them keeping out of sight all day that they intended to attack us before we reached the Dells. The captain said there was no danger of them attacking us; he could take his men and whip all the Indians in the Umatilla valley. So he paid no attention to the warning. Sandy, Prine, Springer, Williams and myself camped in a body to ourselves, a short distance from the main camp. We took it turn about keeping watch that night for the captain only put out two guards and all the rest slept. They were so elated over the victory they achieved over the Indians that they thought they were afraid of them. We saw no Indians that night.

Next morning after we broke camp and started across the sandy hills to Snake river, our little band of five started in advance of the main body and kept it up all the way to the river. We got there about an hour by sun and went into camp. They camped about one hundred and fifty yards from where we were. They got their supper and picketed out their horses and sat down around their campfire talking over the incidents of the last few days till late at night. If they had guards out that night I never knew it. After night awhile we picked up our blankets and went down the river about three hundred yards to a bunch of willows where we intended to camp during the night. We took time about standing guard, for we felt almost certain the Indians would attack us that night.

We had warned the captain time and again to be on his guard and not let the Indians surprise him, but he paid no attention to our advice and traveled right along as if there was not an Indian in a thousand miles of him. He treated the idea of the Indians attacking him with cool contempt. That is the reason we had our camp a little further down the river. After while their camp appeared as quiet as the grave. Many of them who were sleeping so quietly were taking their last sleep. They knew not that the dark shadow of death was hovering over them and that tomorrow's sun many of them would never see.

About three o'clock in the morning the Indians had surrounded their camp, and with yells they rushed into them. The boys jumped to their feet to be met by the Indians in overwhelming numbers, with knife and toma-hawk dealing death on every hand. We started to their rescue as soon as we could. Before we got quite there we met one of the boys who had got through their line run-ning towards us as fast as he could, with three or four Indians after him.

CHAPTER IX.

As soon as they saw us they turned; we fired at them and I don't think they will ever again run another white man. The man who came to us said when they jumped from their blankets it seemed that there were five hundred Indians right in among them. There were many of the boys got their heads split open with tomahawks as they slept. We knew it would not do to stay here till daylight, so we struck out for the foot of the mountain. If we could only get there before the Indians saw us we would stand some chance to get away from them. We reached the mountain, followed along it till we came to a deep gulch where we could hide.

We laid there all day and as soon as night fell we started on for the Dells. We reached there about four o'clock next evening and we were tired and hungry, you bet.

We all went to the hotel to get something to eat. I asked the landlord if Miss Springer was in the parlor. He said she was. He had not seen Mr. Springer up to this time. As soon as he saw him he reached out his hand, exclaiming: "My God, Springer, is this you! How glad I am to see you alive. Come in and see your daughter

who is almost crazy with grief; she thinks you dead."
The pleasure he had in pressing his only child to his
breast, and the sorrow he felt for the sad fate of his wife
and children who had fallen at the hands of the cruel
Indians, I will leave you to guess.

While he was talking to his child I told the landlord
where we found him and how we rescued him, and the
fight the boys had with the Indians, burning up their town,
and how careless the captain had got after we started back,
and how the Indians had attacked them in the night,
killing most of them.

It was sad news for the town, for many of them
lived in town and had families to mourn their untimely
death. The town was wild with excitement all day. The
governor at Salem was asked to send guns and ammunition
as soon as possible. They commenced to raise a company of one hundred men to go and revenge the death
of their comrades. In two or three days two companies of
volunteers came up from the Willamette valley and camped
at the Dells. They had raised seventy-five men and were
waiting for guns. They had elected Charley Williams
Captain, Sandy First Lieutenant and Mr. Springer Second
Lieutenant. Their outfit came on the boat that evening.
The three companies started early next morning up the
river.

It was a sad sight to see Mr. Springer part from his
only child. He told her, while tears were running down
his cheeks, he must go to revenge the death of her dear
mother. So we all shook hands with him and wished
him a safe return to his child.

5

Mr. Prine had made me promise to spend the winter with him, and the next day we started to his cabin on Ochaco creek, one hundred and twenty miles away.

In three days we reached his cabin without any incidents happening worth recording. We went by Mr. Springer's house. It was standing. We looked at the grave of Mrs. Springer; it had not been distturbed.

We found everything at Mr. Prine's cabin as we left it. We had not seen an Indian since we left the Dells, so we thought trouble with them would soon end.

The next day Mr. Prine said we would go out and kill a deer, for we hadn't had any fresh meat for some time. We started early in the morning toward the foot hills and by noon we had killed two, and returned for the ponies to carry them in.

We put in the time hunting until about the last of October, when we heard the boys had got back to the Dells after their long trip after the Indians, and Mr. Prine and I went down to see them and learn what they had done.

We found Mr. Springer and Charley Williams in good health. We asked after Sandy and was told that he was killed with three other boys. They told us they thought there would be no more trouble with the Indians for they had left the country.

Mr. Prine prevailed on Charley Williams to go home with us and spend the winter hunting in the mountains, for there was plenty of deer, bear and elk. There we could have a nice time hunting them. The next morning we packed our ponies and started back.

We went to the post office and Mr. Prine and Charley each got letters — Mr. Prine's from his brother and Charley's from Miss Prine. How glad we were to hear from Mary again, and to hear that she was well and hearty. Mr. Prine begged his brother to visit him in the spring and to bring Mr. Williams and Mr. Carter with him, for he said he owed them a debt of gratitude he would never be able to repay. That Mary had told him so much of these gentlemen that he was anxious to make their acquaintance. Charley would not show his letter for a long time, and when he did I found that he had been corresponding with her. Charley was more anxious to go than we were because Mary was there.

We got back to the Ochaco valley in good spirits. We had many a pleasant day hunting game in the foot hills, and although we had plenty of excitement, Charley was very anxious for spring to come and melt the snow off the mountains.

The snow falls from five to eight feet deep during the winter on the summit. It takes till about the tenth of May before a man can ride across the mountain. That winter to me will long be remembered as one of the most p easant winters of my life. But all pleasures have their end, and so the winter soon passed and we were preparing to start across the mountains.

CHAPTER X.

We started the ninth day of May. We had some difficulty in crossing the streams and found the snow on the summit of the mountain from one to two feet deep. We crossed over in safety and found the Willamette valley covered with wild flowers. Oh, what a change!— from deep snow to a flower bed. We learned it was about thirty miles from the foot of the mountain to where Mr. Prine lived. We camped there that night, and early in the morning we started. About the middle of the afternoon we came in sight of Mr. Prine's house. Mary met us at the door and gave us a hearty welcome to her father's house. She took us into the parlor where her father and mother were sitting and introduced us to them and told them we were the two young men that rescued her from the Indians. Mr. Prine gave us a warm welcome to his house and told us to make his house our home as long as we staid in the valley. Mary's brother soon came in and she introduced us to him. We asked him to tell us what had happened to him that morning he left his sister and went to hunt his horses. He said: "I started down the river, for I thought they might have started back home. I had gone about two miles, when to my left near the foothills, I saw two or three Indians. They saw me about the same time. Gathering their bows and arrows, they started for me and I broke and ran. They shot several arrows at me and followed me several miles down the river, but I outran them. It is about ten miles from the Mountain house, at the edge of the valley, where sister and I were camped. When I reached the house I found four men there. I told them about my horses getting loose and when I started that morning to find them how the Indians had shot at me and followed me quite a distance. By night we had a company of twenty men that would be ready to start early in the morning to see what had become of Mary. About three o'clock in the morning they started, and at sun-up they got to the place where we had camped. We found the wagon there but Mary was gone. We hunted over the mountains and hills for miles around but saw no sign of her, nor anything that would lead us to any conclusion as to what had become of her, but we thought the Indians had carried her off. We hunted there for three days without seeing an Indian. At the end of the third day we went back to the valley. I had found one of my horses and took it and started home to tell my father and mother the sad story of Mary's disappearance.

In a day or two we heard of the outbreak of the Indians in eastern Oregon; then we all believed that Mary had been taken prisoner by the Indians, unless she was dead.

The governor had called for volunteers. I intended to go but the day before I was going to start to town to join the company Mary came home. The joy we realized in seeing her at home again well and hearty, can never be told."

How happily the days were passing away with us! But I soon found, to my sorrow, that I was about to lose my dear friend and partner. We had been there about two weeks, when one morning Charley came and told me he was the happiest man in the world, for Mary had promised to marry him and he was going to ask Mr. Prine that day for his daughter's hand. The wedding was to take place two weeks from that day.

I told them that I intended to start to California in a few days, but they persuaded me to stay till after the wedding.

The time soon rolled around when the two were made one, and a happier couple I never saw.

Tears came into their eyes when I bade them farewell and started on my journey to California.

CHAPTER XI.

How sad and lonely the journey seemed to me without Charley, for he had been my bosom friend for over two years.

When I bade Charley and his wife farewell, and started on my long journey to California, my heart was sad; for I was leaving those who had become dear to me through the trials and hardships that we had passed through together during the last year. So it was that I bade them a long farewell, and started on my lonely road to prospect for gold in the wild mountains and deep gulches of California. There was nothing to disturb the loneliness of my journey until the evening of the third day. I stopped at a house on a little stream called Grave creek. This stream had its origin in the foothills near the Cascade range of mountains, and ran in a westerly direction until its waters emptied into the Pacific ocean. After supper my host and I lighted our pipes and went out on the veranda to smoke.

I found he was a jolly fellow and very talkative, so I asked him why this was called Grave Creek House. He said it was a long story, but if I would be patient and listen, he would tell it to me. I told him I would be more than pleased to hear the story, so he began :

"A long time ago, before any white men had been in this part of the country, the Umpqua Indians owned all this valley. There was a large tribe of them at that time. They and the Rogue River Indians were great allies. For a long time they had visited each other, and had grand contests in the use of their war implements with the young chiefs of their tribes.

The old chief, Oso, had a beautiful daughter by the name of Sunflower, who was the pride of the tribe. She was tall and graceful with her long black hair falling below her waist. She was loved by the tribe as few women were ever loved before. There was one of the young chiefs from Rogue River, who fell in love with her, and offered the old chief, her father, fifty ponies for her. Oso went to Sunflower and told her what the young chief had offered for her, if she would go and live in his wigwam. With a dark frown upon her face, she told her father she would rather die than to live in a wigwam with a Rogue River Indian. Oso went and told the young chief what Sunflower had said, and from that day, there grew a coldness between the two tribes, that ripened into hatred, and ended in a bloody war.

The young chief that fell in love with Sunflower, got about twenty warriors to go with him to steal her away from her tribe. They had laid in ambush for several days, when late one evening, they saw her coming towards them, looking at the golden sunset, and not thinking of danger. Suddenly the young chief sprang up from his place of concealment, and caught her in his arms. She screamed with all her might, but once only;

for he put his hand over her mouth and ran with all his might to where their ponies were tied. An old squaw heard the cry, and saw them carrying Sunflower off. She gave the alarm, and in a few moments about thirty warriors were in hot pursuit. They traveled about two miles before they overtook the fleeing party, and then occurred one of the bloodiest battles that was ever fought with the same number of men.

All of the Rogue River Indians were killed, but the young chief, and eighteen of the Umpquas were killed or wounded. When the chief saw that he was going to lose Sunflower, he tried to kill her, but was foiled in that. He fought like a demon until all his warriors were down but two, then he mounted his pony, and rode off like a whirlwind. Several of the Umpquas followed him for miles but could not overtake him. They then turned with sad hearts to the place where the fight occurred, and took Sunflower and the wounded back to the village, where, under the loving care of Sunflower, the wounded rapidly recovered and were soon ready to start on the war path again. During the following year, many warriors on both sides were killed." My host pointed to a large knoll half a mile up the creek from his house. "Do you see that?" I told him that I did. "There," he said, "is where they buried their warriors that were slain in recovering Sunflower from the Rogue River Indians."

"The first settlers came here in 1848. There were two families; one of them settled this place, and I bought him out in 1851, and they took a claim higher up the creek. They gave this place the name of Grave Creek House on account of the Indians being buried out there." It being late, we walked back to the house and went to bed, but not to sleep, for I was thinking of Sunflower, and wondering what had become of her. The night passed wearily by, and in the morning, I asked my host if he knew what had become of Sunflower. He lighted his pipe and sat down on the porch. " She lived to be old," he said, " and was loved by all the whites that lived in the valley." "Did she ever marry?" " No, she lived almost entirely among the whites, and the children learned to love her as they did their own grandmother. When they saw her coming, they would run to meet her, and taking her by the hand, would lead her into the house. About one year ago, she died, and I think there were more white people went to see her laid away by the side of her father, than were ever at an Indian burial before ; and many an eye was wet with tears, for she was a Christian, and tried to do good all the days of her life. May she rest in peace."

" What became of the young chief ? " " Two years after he tried to kill Sunflower, he was killed in a fight with the Umpquas." About nine o'clock in the morning I bade my host goodbye, and the next night I stopped with a man named Harris, living about thirty miles from Grave Creek. Mr. Harris, who was about forty years of age, had a wife and two children ; a boy twelve years old, and a girl nine. Mrs. Harris was a small woman, weight, about ninety pounds, with dark eyes and auburn hair, that fell in ringlets over her neck. She was a very pleasant talker. There was a young Indian about the place, sixteen years of age. I asked them where he belonged? They told me he had been living with them three years. I asked them if they were not afraid the Indians would break out some time and kill them all, living so far away from any neighbors, the nearest house being three miles away. I told them the young Indian they were raising might turn out to be a " rattlesnake," and bite them when they were least expecting it. They laughed at me, and said they didn't think there was any danger; but how sadly they were mistaken, as the sequel will show.

I passed a pleasant night with them, and in the morning bade them goodbye, never more to see Mr. Harris or his boy. Late in the day I got to Jacksonville, a mining camp in southern Oregon, now one of the finest fruit valleys in the state of Oregon. None of the valley was cultivated at that time, except a few garden spots ; but now it looks like a Garden of Eden. I stayed there a few days, then crossed the mountains into California.

The day before I reached Yreka, I fell in company with two young men, who had come up from the Willamette valley. They were going to try their luck in the gold fields of California. At night we camped on the east side of the mountain that overlooked the town of Yreka, sitting in a little valley right at the foot of the mountain, and near a little stream by the same name. One of the boys was small, the other tall, long-legged, and about twenty years of age. He said he would go and get our horses, while the other fellow and I got breakfast. So he started out to find them, for we had turned them loose the evening before.

We got breakfast, and had eaten, and were wondering what had kept him so long, when we saw him coming, bare-headed, and running with all his might. When he came up to us, we saw he was very pale. His mouth was wide open, but he never spoke a word. I asked him what was the matter, but it was some time before he could speak. When he did speak, all he said was: "Bear! bear! bear!" I asked where, and he never spoke, but pointed toward the top of the mountain. I saw he had lost quite a bunch of hair from the side of his head, and that he had, in some way, lost the seat of his pants. No wonder the poor fellow was scared. After much coaxing, we got him to tell us the circumstance. On the west side of the mountain there was a small patch of grass. Not finding the ponies, he started around the west side of the mountain, and was passing close to the grassy plot, where there was a number of chaparral bushes, when a large bear jumped up and struck him on the head and knocked him head-long down the mountain, which was very steep at that place. When the man fell, the bear jumped and grabbed the seat of his pants and tore it off as he went down the mountain. At last we succeeded in getting him to show us where it happened, though we could not get him within fifty yards of the place. I had a small rifle, and the other man had a Colt's revolver. We went to the place, and saw where the bear had gone down the side of the mountain to a thick bunch of chaparral. We had never seen one of those big fellows, so we were not afraid of it any more than we would have been of a wild hog. We followed its track down the mountain, until it entered a thick bush. The boy said he would follow its track through the bushes if I would go around and shoot it as it came out on the other side. I had scarcely time to reach the other side, when I heard the old pistol bang. Then I heard the bushes crackling like a wagon and team was running away through them. In a second I saw the bear coming. My! It looked like an elephant. It was coming straight towards where I was standing, and I felt that I was stretching up about an inch taller at every breath. If it hadn't been for a bunch of chaparral that stood right in front of me, I don't know how tall I might have got. It was a little open to the right of the bushes, and I hoped the bear would make that turn ; if it didn't I couldn't stay there any longer, for I felt as if I was standing on nettles. No fellow could stand on them long, when there was a bear right in front of him. My prayer was answered. I think my hat was at least four inches above the crown of my head, when the bear turned to the right. It passed within about forty yards of where I was standing and, as it got a little past me, I fired, and the ball struck him just behind the shoulder. It stopped and snapped at its side, looked in all directions, but did not see me ; for I was standing l ke a statue. Then it took down the side of the mountain. By this time we had become very thirsty. It was nearly a quarter of a mile down the mountain to the town, so we went and got a drink. I met a young lawyer named Tyler, and told him about shooting a bear on the side of the mountain, pointing up to where I had last seen the bear. He ran and got a gun, and said he would go with me. We went in a hurry back to the mountain, and soon found where the bear was lying. I bursted two caps at him, but my gun would not go off. I picked powder in the tube, and finally fired it, then loaded it again. The bear got up and started along the side of the mountain, which terminated in a sharp ridge on top. By the time we reached the top, there were about fifty men at the foot of the mountain. They could see the bear in the bushes, almost at the top of the ridge. The man that was with me kept saying, " If we get in a fight with the bear, don't you run." We could tell from the way the men were hallooing, and pointing below, that the bear was about one hundred yards ahead of us. There were three or four small oak trees about thirty feet high near where we were standing. As we ran towards the bushes where the bear was, my companion said, "Now don't you run ! " We went about fifteen steps further, and saw the bear. I walked up within forty feet of where the bear was standing, looking right up at me. I took aim at his forehead, fired, and he sank to the ground. Then I turned to look at the young man who was with me. Where do you think I saw him ? At the top of one of those little oaks. I started to go down where the bear was, when the men below yelled, " You fool, the bear will kill you ! He is not dead ! " I went down and got astraddle of it, and pulled it over on one side, before any of them would come within fifty yards of it. I went down in town and got a wagon and team, while the men pulled the bear down the mountain. We loaded it in the wagon, took it down to the creek and dressed it, then took it up in town to the butcher shop and weighed it. It weighed eight hundred pounds, and sold for sixty cents a pound as fast as the butcher could weigh it out.

CHAPTER XII.

In the morning after killing the bear, I met two miners that had a claim near the lower crossing on Hamburg creek, about ten miles from Yreka. We had to climb over a high mountain to get to the creek. I hired to the men and went over to work. I found that the mountains were so high that the sun only shown on their claim about two hours during the day. I sold them my mule for one hundred and twenty-five dollars, and worked for them three months. Their claim did not pay very well, so two other men and I bought a bar a little above theirs, and went to digging a ditch to lead the water on to the back of the bar, so we could sluice the dirt off into the creek. The ditch would have to be about two hundred and fifty yards long, and there were places that it would have to be fifteen feet deep. We went to work and had it dug about one hundred and fifty yards, and were in the deepest part of the ditch. We had a plank fixed about seven feet down from the top, so the men that were digging in the bottom of the ditch could pitch the dirt from the bottom to the board, and one man could stand on the board and throw the dirt out at the top. I had been standing on the board about two hours throwing the dirt out. I became thirsty and got out to get me a drink of water, and was back within five feet of the ditch, when it caved in, about fifty yards of it. It had entirely closed together up to the top, and was only about two and a half feet wide, and twelve feet deep, where the two men were covered up. I ran up the creek hallooing as loud as I could, and in less than twenty minutes, thirty or forty miners were there with their picks and shovels, and went to work in earnest to dig out the men. It must have been about two hours before we got to the old man. As soon as we got the dirt off his head, he said, "Hurry, and pull me out." We had to dig close down to his feet before we could lift him out. We asked where the other man was working, and he said about twenty feet below him. "But you need not be in a hurry, for I know he is dead." So after getting the old man out, we sat down to rest a moment, then went to work again digging for the other. It took us some time to dig to him, and when we found him, we thought he was dead, for he was black in the face and as limber as a rag. We carried him down to our cabin and laid him on his blankets. The doctor commenced working with him, and in about two hours he began to show signs of life. The doctor stayed all night with him, and the next morning he was able to talk a little. In six weeks the man was able to go to work again.

I sold my claim there and went back to Yreka, and bought a claim on Chinese Gulch. There being no water in the gulch during the summer, we had to dig our dirt

7

and pile it up and wait for the rains in winter, so we could wash out the gold from the dirt and gravel. In my claim I had to dig shafts about sixteen to twenty feet, to get down to the bed rock where the gold was found, and then run tunnels off from the main shafts and carry the dirt back to the shafts and windlass it out in big buckets. It was in the spring of 1855, when I was working there. Some time in September, news came that the Indians had killed two men on the trail that runs from Yreka over Scott's mountain to a mining camp on Scott river. The next morning we heard that they had killed seven miners and the butcher that lived on the river. The miners raised a company and followed their trail over the mountains, and saw them enter the reservations on Bear creek in Oregon.

Captain Smith of the regular army had charge of the reservation there at that time, with about one hundred soldiers. The boys followed the Indians right to Captain Smith's, told him what the Indians had done, and how many men they had killed. He said he did not believe they did it—the boys said they did, some sharp words were exchanged, and they told the captain they had come for the Indians and were going to have them, and started towards the Indian camp. Smith wheeled the cannon around on them and ordered them back, and told them if they did not obey he would open fire upon them. He said he knew his Indians never did the killing, that they were peaceable Indians, and would do anything for him that he asked of them. So the boys had to come back without an Indian. About two weeks after they got back, two Indians came into Yreka to buy ammunition.   Some one got suspicious and had them arrested.   They were asked if they had any guns, and they said no.

Just at that time a miner came in from Willow Creek and said he saw them go into the brush over there with two guns.   Two men were ordered to go and search for the guns.   They were gone but a short time when they returned with the guns in their hands.   The miners took the Indians away from the officers, bound their hands behind them, put them into a wagon, and started out west of town to a big pine tree, where a limb had grown out from the main body of the tree about ten feet from the ground.   They drove the wagon under the tree, put a rope around the necks of the Indians, and threw the other end over the limb.   One of them called out in the Indian dialect that he wanted to see his chief before they killed him.   One of the boys answered, "You will see your chief before you are ready to, you red devil," and grabbing the rope, began pulling. They drove the wagon from under the tree and left them hanging, and went back to town.

CHAPTER XIII.

In about one month all the Indians had left the reservation where Captain Smith was, and joined the Rogue River Indians. All the Indians in southern Oregon went on the war path, and began killing all the defenseless men, women and children they could find, and burned up everything, even the women and children. They would surround their houses, bar the doors and set fire to the house. All those that could get away, 'flocked to the cities for safety. Along the line between Oregon and California, there was but one house in a distance of sixty miles. The Indians had run off all the stock, and burned everything before them. Almost every man that was able to carry a gun, was out fighting the Indians. This war began in the fall of 1855, and continued through the summer of 1856. Early in the spring of 1856, I started back to Oregon. As I was crossing the Siskiyou mountain and was going down on the north side, I came upon a wagon, where four yoke of oxen had been hitched to it. The off ox of each yoke had been shot down, while the near ox of each yoke was standing there by its dead mate. I looked around and saw, out by the side of the road, two men that had been killed, and were cut almost to pieces. I rode back to the

Mountain house and got three men. We came back, loosed the oxen, and took the mangled corpses down to the house and buried them. They were so badly cut to pieces that we could not identify them. The next day I crossed Rogue river, and traveled about twelve miles to where the volunteers had their winter quarters. About thirty soldiers were quartered here. The captain made me stay all night with him. He asked me where I was going. I told him I was going up to Oregon. "Not alone?" he said. I told him yes. He said it would be almost impossible for me to reach the Umpqua canon alone, for the Indians were killing men along the road almost every day. It was sixty miles from there to the canon. That evening the captain told me how the Indians came up to Mr. Harris's house one morning early, and called him to the door and shot him down. He would have fallen out of the door, but Mrs. Harris caught him and closed the door. She began to scream, but Mr. Harris told her not to take on so, but to get the gun and shoot out of the window at them. She said she had never fired a gun and did not know how to load it. Mr. Harris showed her how to load and shoot, and she shot out of the window at them all day. About three o'clock in the afternoon Mr. Harris died. He told her a few moments before to keep shooting at them as long as she lived. She said the Indian boy who had been living with them, was the one who called Mr. Harris to the door. Sometime during the day, they shot the little girl through the fleshy part of her arm. Just before Mr. Harris was called to the door, they had sent the little boy to the potato patch to get some potatoes for breakfast, and they never saw him again. Mrs. Harris kept shooting at them till they left, a little before sundown. There was a slough just back of the house, that was thickly covered with rose bushes, and as soon as it got dark, she took her little girl and went out there and hid in the rose bushes, and stayed there all night and till about nine o'clock the next morning.

She was afraid to leave for she thought the Indians might be around watching for her. About that time she heard horses' feet coming along the road, which made her tremble, for she thought it might be Indians. She peeped out from among the bushes, and, to her joy, saw it was a company of soldiers. She called to them, and taking her little girl ran toward them. She told her sad story to them and they all went to the house where lay Mr. Harris, dead. In his agony he had crawled up and down the stairs, for they were bloody from bottom to top. It was, indeed, a sad sight, but such was the fate of many during that cruel Indian war. The soldiers made a rough box, put Mr. Harris in it and buried him in a little fir grove near the house.

The soldiers took Mrs. Harris and her little girl back with them to their camp and there they secured a wagon and team and took them on to Jacksonville and left them there, sad, and broken hearted. As the soldiers were starting back, she cried to them with a sad wail: "For God's sake, find my boy! My poor boy! What has become of him?" Then fell back exhausted to the floor

After telling me this, he said: "Were you ever ac-quainted with Mr. Wagoner and family?" "Yes," I said, "I have taken dinner there several times." "You will never take dinner with them again," said he. "Why not?" Then he told me: "One day Mr. Wagoner went to Jacksonville—I think it was in November—and while he was gone the Indians surrounded his house, barred the doors, set fire to the house, and burned Mrs. Wagoner and the two girls in the house. When Mr. Wagoner returned, all that was left to him of that happy wife and two daughters was the smouldering ruins of the house and the ghastly sight of the charred bodies of wife and daughters. That must have filled his heart with anguish, for that morning he left them well and happy and now what was left of his loved ones was horrible to look upon. While looking upon their ghastly remains, he vowed he would not rest day nor night until he avenged their cruel death. He then returned to Jacksonville and told his sad story and began raising a company to go and fight the Indians; but before he got the company or-ganized he took to drinking, and from that to gambling, and from the best information I can get, he never fired a gun at an Indian during the war."

We ate our breakfast early next morning and the captain detailed eight men to go with me as a guard to the canon.

That night we camped in an old stable about ten miles from the canon. The house had been burned down. There was a Dutchman with us, whose watch came on about four o'clock in the morning. He was standing just

inside an old shed back of the stable which we were in.
He had not been standing there more than half an hour
when he spoke to the boys, and said: "Mine Got! I see
someting oud yonder; it is raising itself up a leetle! Boys
its gitting up! So pig as von tam Injun; I shoots!"
Bang! went his gun, and you just ought to have heard an
old sow squeal. Then the boys began to laugh at him.
"Vell boys, you may laugh yust as much as you tam
please, but I lets no tam sow bite me." Then the boys
roared with laughter, and there was no more sleep in
camp for us that night.

We got up early and had our breakfast by sunrise.
I told the boys I thought I could go the rest of the way
alone without any danger, so I started on my road and
the boys returned to their camp.

The canon was a narrow place where a little stream
ran through the Umpqua mountains down into the valley.
A man in passing through the canon had to follow the
bed of the creek all the way, for it was solid rock on each
side, and was from fifty to five hundred feet high, and
about eight miles in length. The night before I got
there it had rained heavily in the mountains so the creek
was booming through the canon like a mill race. In
places the water would come half way up on my horse's
sides and it would be all he could do to keep on his feet.
At the mouth of the canon where it enters into the
Umpqua valley, it turns to the right and pitches down
over the rocks like a whirlpool. Just above where it turns
down the hill is the old crossing, and about ten feet
above they had started to build a bridge and had three

bents put up about ten feet apart, with an approach on each side about six feet long. They had two planks two by eight inches lying side by side across the frame work. When I got there I saw that it would be almost impossible to ford the stream so I did not know just what to do as I was afraid to stay there long. I got off and tried to lead my horse across the bridge on the planks but he would not budge a foot. I tried quite awhile to get him onto the plank, but it was no go. Then I thought I would try riding him over and as soon as I got on him and started him he walked straight across the bridge. I think I was scared ten times as bad as the horse, for I don't think I drew a single breath while crossing. In the center of the bridge it was fifteen feet down to the water.

I rode on down to the Canon house and stayed there all night. The landlord fed my horse wheat that night and the next morning he was foundered so badly that I could scarcely get him out of the stable. I thought it would be better to exercise him than let him stand in the stable, so I started on my journey.

The roads in the spring of the year were almost impassable. It would have been almost impossible to have got over them with a team and wagon at that time. So what little traveling was done was on horseback.

There was a narrow path beat down in the center of the road about one foot wide, and if you got out of that, you would sink into the mud almost to your knees. I had ridden about five miles and could hardly get my horse along, so I got off and drove him before me. I had walked seven miles, and was pretty tired, and my

horse seemed rested, so I took him by the tail and called
to him to stop, and stepped outside of the trail into the
mud, when my pony started off in a trot. I didn't
like that very well, but it was just the same to the
pony. I soon caught up with him and tried it again,
but the pony had not forgotten his advantage over me,
and away he went again. I now began to get mad, but
it did no good, for I had to walk behind him till about
two o'clock in the afternoon. By this time I was
thoroughly mad. I looked ahead of me and saw a man
coming, then I smiled and thought, "Now, old fellow, I
have got you!" When the man got near enough, I
called to him: "For God's sake catch my horse. He
has been making me walk all day!" The man laughed
heartily as he took the horse by the bridle. He asked
me how far I had walked. I told him. "Well," said
he, "you have had a pretty hard day's work." I told
him if he had walked it, he would certainly think so. I
asked him how far it was to the Calapooya mountain.
He said it was eight miles. I mounted my horse and
started off on a trot, and kept it up for miles, and
stopped that night at the foot of the mountain, and the
next evening reached Eugene City at the head of the
Willamette valley. It was late in the evening when I
got there, and I asked the landlord if he could give me
a bed, and he said yes, but he had only one unoccupied.
I·went to bed, and in a short time the landlord came
and asked if I would let a man sleep with me. I told
him I did not like to sleep with a stranger, but to
bring him up and let me look him over. I was sleeping

upstairs in a large room that contained several beds, all of them occupied. The landlord soon came back with a boy about sixteen years old. I looked at him and answered, "Yes, he may sleep with me." I lay for sometime with my back towards him, then turned over and asked him if he was asleep. "No," he said. Then I told him the reason that I did not like to sleep with strangers. I said I had been down in California and had a good deal of trouble, that I came very near killing two men, that if I got to dreaming and began to grit my teeth, for him to wake me as soon as possible, or I might hurt him. While I was telling him that, I could hear the men snoring all around the room. He laughed at me and said he was not afraid. "All right," said I, "but I never sleep with a stranger without telling him, so if I hurt him I am not to blame. If you will just shake me I will soon wake up. I contracted the habit while in California, of gritting my teeth." I turned over on my back and was soon fast asleep. I had slept sometime when I was awakened by the boy shaking me and calling, "Stranger! Stranger!" "What's up!" said I. "Why, you are gritting your teeth like the devil," said he. The noise woke up all the men in the room, and they commenced laughing at him, and kept it up till morning. Occasionally some one would call out, "Say, young fellow, are you asleep? I would not sleep with that man for a thousand dollars." Then they would break out laughing, and so the night passed, and in the morning we got up early and went down to breakfast. The

landlord asked what was the matter with us all last
night.   One of the men told him the joke, and they all
took a hearty laugh but the boy.   It was no laughing
matter for him.   After breakfast I bade them goodbye,
and started down the valley to where I had a brother
living, and had ridden about six miles, when I met my
old friend Charley Williams and his wife going to town.
I was glad to meet them, jumped off my horse and ran
up to shake hands with them.   It seems to me they
asked me a thousand questions before I had time to
answer one.   They wanted to know where I had been
and where I was going.   I told them I was going down
the valley to my brother's.   They persuaded me to go
back to town with them and then to go home with them
and stay a few days.

When we reached home and Mrs. Williams had got
us something to eat, they both came and sat down close
to me and asked me to tell them about my trip to
California, and all I knew about the Indian war that had
been going on in southern Oregon.   I told them something about my trip, then I told them how the Indians
were burning every house they came across, and sometimes the women and children in them.   Charley said if
he was foot loose, he would go back with me and help
fight them, for they were the meanest Indians that ever
lived.   He asked me if I was going back there soon.   I
told him if we could raise a company of volunteers, I
would go.   I stayed with them two days, then went down
the valley to my brother's, stayed with them about two
weeks, and heard that they were raising a company of

volunteers at Brownsville, about ten miles below where my brother lived. It was almost impossible to get up a company, as all the able-bodied men were already gone.

CHAPTER XIV.

To every man who would volunteer to go and fight the Indians, and furnish his own horse and gun, the Governor offered to pay four dollars a day, for three months, or as long as war continued. I joined the company. As soon as we got fifty men, we went out to Eugene City, and were mustered into service. As soon as we could possibly get ready, we went to the scene of action. The third day we encamped in sight of Roseburg, which is in the Umpqua valley. The next day we traveled southwest to a valley called Commercial Prarie. About twenty miles from Roseburg we found the Indians had burned most of the houses in the valley, and run off all the stock. We followed their trail which ran in a southern direction over the mountains to the big bend in Rogue river, a distance of sixty or seventy miles. Their path which was well beaten, we followed without difficulty.

The second day we traveled over the rugged Ball mountain and late in the evening reached the foot, where we found a small stream of water with considerable timber growing along its banks, and here we camped for the night.

It was a beautiful place to camp about one hundred and fifty feet from the creek, and here the Indian signs were fresh, so we kept a sharp lookout for them. My turn to go on guard was about nine o'clock at night. The man I relieved stood right in the trail near the creek. The corporal brought a lantern with him, for it was as dark a night as I have ever seen. We could not see our hands before our eyes. When I got to where he was standing I saw out to one side of the trail a large fir tree and as soon as they left me I stepped out to the tree and got it between me and the campfires, for some of them were burning brightly. I asked the guard before he left if he had heard any noise during his watch. He said he had heard a noise several times on the opposite side of the creek, pointing toward the foot of the mountain. I think I had been standing by the tree about an hour when I heard something coming up the trail toward me. I knew if it was an Indian he could not see me for it was so dark I could not see anything right before my eyes. It would walk a few steps and then stop a moment, then it would take a few more steps and stop again. I was almost sure it was an Indian and I thought he was looking for the man on guard. It came on, stopping occasionally, until it stood right before me; then I said: "One more step and I will shoot." It stopped a moment then turned out of the trail and came towards me. The hair began to raise on the top of my head. I tried to make no sound, but I feared the beating of my heart could be heard ten feet away. Every step it would take I would say the next step I will shoot, but I let it come right up to within a few yards of me then I lowered my gun until I thought it would hit a man in the pit of the stomach, and fired. It gave one big grunt and ran off down through the woods towards the creek, and I ran back to the camp. I ran right over the boys lying on the ground and never stopped until I got on the other side of the camp. As I ran through the camp one of the boys stuck his head out from under his blanket and asked, "What is the matter?" The others said: "Keep your d——d head down or you will get it shot off." The captain came to me and asked me what I had shot at? I told him I thought it was a bear and if I had crippled it it would have followed me into camp and the first one who raised his head would have had it snapped off. Then there would have been a stampede among the boys. Early in the morning some of the boys went down to where I had stood and there right in front of my tracks was a big bear track. You could stand in my tracks and touch the bear's tracks with the end of your gun.

The next evening after a hard day's travel over the mountains we reached the bend in the Rogue river. Three hundred volunteers had been fighting the Indians all that day about one mile above the bend. A few shots were fired during the night, but in the morning not an Indian was to be seen. We supposed they had gone down the valley.

Early in the morning we were ordered to commence building a picket fort, which was to be fifty feet wide by two hundred feet long. We dug a ditch two feet wide by three feet deep, then we cut fir logs twelve feet long and split them in the center and set them on end in the ditch close together. This we called a picket fort. While we were building the fort two spies were sent down the river to see if they could find any signs of Indians. They re· turned at night and reported that they had found an Indian village about fifteen miles down the river and had seen where they had been traveling up and down the river, and they believed the entire band of Indians went down there last night. So the company I belonged to was detailed to start at ten o'clock that night and go around below the village. We went around over the mountains and reached our position about an hour before sunrise. Our orders were to wait till we should see the main body of soldiers coming over the mountain, which was about five miles up the river from the Indian village, and then we were to attack the Indians, while the main body came up in the rear, and we would have them between two fires. It was about nine o'clock when we saw the boys coming. The Indians saw them at the same time and gave the war whoop and it seemed to me that five hundred Indians raised out of the ground with their guns in hand ready to meet the enemy.

„By the time the boys came up the old war chief, John, had called them all together and was talking to them when we opened fire. We fought them about two hours, then the Indians jumped into the river and swam to the other side. We killed several in the water. As soon as they got across they took to the mountains and we saw no more of them.

8

About one week after this, while scouting down the river, we surprised a small band of them, kille several and the others escaped into the mountains.

At the same time Old John and Olympia had Captain Smith and his soldiers surrounded on a little knoll about twenty miles below. They had them surrounded for thirty-six hours and would have killed the last one of them if Captain Auger had not come up and routed the Indians. Just before Captain Auger fired into the Indians Old John, who could talk good English, told his men to quit wasting ammunition and wait till night, then they would go into the camp and tomahawk all the soldiers except Smith. They intended to hang him. Thirty-seven of Smith's men had been killed or wounded before the Indians were routed by Captain Auger. I went all over the knoll where the soldiers were encamped. There was a fir tree about three feet in diameter that had fallen across the side of the knoll about fifty yards from where the soldiers had dug a pit and thrown up the dirt for breastworks. Part of the soldiers had got on one side of the log and the Indians had crawled up on the other side. The ground was as slick on both sides as if hogs had been wallowing there for a month. The Indians killed four soldiers at the log. They would throw stones and sticks over the log and when the soldiers would raise their heads the Indians would shoot them. Several of our boys called out: "Captain, where are good Indians that you loved so well last fall? Are they the ones who stood guard over you the other night?" He swore like a trooper and said he would have all of us arrested. Our captain dared him to lay hands on any of us.

At three o'clock in the afternoon we started down the river and after traveling about twenty miles reached a place where the Indians had made a dam of rock, at each side of which was a space about two feet wide. They had built the dam to catch salmon as they come up the river from the ocean. They made willow nets and placed them above the openings in the dam, as the salmon would go into them. The fish were dressed and laid out to dry for winter use. This dam was about twenty miles from where the river empties into the Pacific ocean.

The river at its mouth was one mile wide. About half a mile up the beach from the mouth of the river is a place they call Gold beach. There had been considerable mining going on at this place, but when the Indians broke out they killed several of the miners, burned the town and drove the rest of the people out of the country. At this place were three companies of volunteers.

We stayed here about three weeks and during that time the Indians commenced coming in and giving themselves up. Captain Smith with his regulars came down about one week after we arrived; then we were ordered to turn all the prisoners over to him. In less than one month about fifteen hundred Indians had come in and given themselves up to Captain Smith and were taken up to Port Offord and put on the reservation in the Yanhill country in Oregon.

CHAPTER XV.

We were ordered back to Eugene City and there disbanded.

There I learned for the first time of the disappearance of Mrs. Harris. About three weeks after the death of her husband she received a letter from a friend living twelve miles from Jacksonville in the little valley called Butte Prairie. She took a horse one day and started up there to see her friends, and that was the last they saw of her. Her friends scoured the country for her in every direction but no trace of her could be found. Some thought the Indians had killed her, but they soon dropped that notion for not an Indian had been seen in that country for a long time, and if she had been drowned in the river her horse would have been found. What had become of Mrs. Harris was the talk of the entire neighborhood, when I reached Jacksonville.

I staid in Jacksonville about two weeks and during that time I came across an old friend I had met in California in the fall of 1854 by the name of Allwood. This is the way I got acquainted with him: I was at Yreka one Saturday night and had stepped into the Eldorado saloon to see a man. A big rough looking man was at the bar talking very loud and angrily. I stopped and was listening to him, when he turned round to me and said: "Stranger, take a drink with me." "No," said I, "I never drink." "You ———— tenderfoot, you shall drink with me." Just at that time Mr. Allwood stepped up to him and said in a pleasant voice: "If that boy doesn't want to drink you had better let him alone." The man turned around and looked the speaker in the face and said: "It is none of your ———— business, and if you don't go away you will get your face slapped."

As quick as lightning the stranger pulled his pistol out of his pocket and thrust it in the face of the man and said, "What is that?" The man skulked out of the room without saying another word. Then I stepped up to the stranger and asked him to go home with me and stay all night, for I wanted to talk with him. He went and stayed two days. I asked where he was mining. He said he was no miner, he had come down on a visit to a friend that was mining on Green Horn creek. I then asked where he lived, and he told me he had been trapping in the mountains near the head waters of Klamath and Rogue rivers, on the east side of the mountain. He had been trapping there for years. When we met in Jacksonville, I was very glad to see him. He was stopping at the Eagle House, and he asked me to come to his room that evening, for he wanted to have a long talk with me about Mrs. Harris's disappearance. I had commenced talking to him about her, and was telling how her husband was killed and was describing her to him, when some one called to him and said he wanted to speak with him a moment. As he turned to the man, he asked me to be sure and come around to his room that evening. I strolled around over town till supper time, and after supper, I took a smoke, and then went to the hotel where Mr. Allwood was staying. I went up stairs o his room and knocked at the door. "Come in," he said. I opened the door and went in. He said, "I have been waiting for you," and getting up he went to the door and locked it. "I don't want to be disturbed in our conversation tonight." He then asked me to tell him about Mrs. Harris, and describe her as near as possible. After I had given him the description, he sat looking at the floor a long time, then he raised his head and said, "I have seen that woman somewhere." At last he exclaimed, "I have it! Early last spring I set some traps on this side of the mountains on a little stream where I had seen some beaver signs. Early one morning I took my gun and started over the mountain to look at my traps. I had reached the summit and was starting down the mountain, when I heard horses' feet. Stepping behind some bushes I waited for them to come up. I wanted to see who they were. In a short time they came up, and I saw three men and one woman. Two of the men were as tough looking customers as ever I saw. The other was a medium sized man, well dressed, rather dark complexion, and about twenty-five years old. One of the rough men was leading the woman's horse. The woman was small, with long curly hair, and looked pale and careworn. I am sure now it was Mrs. Harris, and I am also sure I have seen that young man before.

I think I know who he is. If I am correct in my suspicions, his father is the leader of a band of robbers, whose stronghold is in the mountains somewhere." I asked Mr. Allwood when he was going back to the mountains. He said, "In a day or two, and I want you to go with me, for I think we can find out all about Mrs. Harris. I am sure that was her I saw riding that day with those men." I said I would go and asked him who he thought the men were. "It's a long story but I will tell you in as few words as I can. In 1849, I crossed the plains and landed in lower California, and stopped at San Bernardino. While there, I got acquainted with a man keeping a saloon by the name of Mack Duvall. Several men had been robbed at his saloon, and two men had disappeared very mysteriously. The last that was seen of them, they were in his saloon, and he was suspected of putting them out of the way, so they began watching him. He always had a rough looking gang around him, and often he would be gone for two or three weeks at a time, and no one knew where he went. He was married to a half Mexican woman, and she ran the business while he was gone. The stage was robbed between Los Angeles and San Bernardino one evening. Mack was seen in the neighborhood where the robbery took place, the same day, by two men who knew him. The next day there was a search warrant got out, and Mack's house was searched, and several articles were found which were in the stage when it was robbed. He was tried and convicted, and sentenced to eight years in the penitentiary. The sheriff and two deputies started with him to San Quentin. On the second day of their journey, they were attacked by a band of outlaws, and the prisoner was taken from them. Nothing was heard from him for a long time. The next that was heard of him was in Arizona. They got so bold down there that the soldiers got after them. Late one evening the soldiers came upon them while they were eating supper. A hard battle was fought in which several men were killed on both sides. Duvall saw his men falling around him, and darted off into some bushes where their horses were tied, and mounting, he rode away followed by a shower of bullets. I never heard of him after this, until I saw him at Goose Lake early this spring. That young man that was with Mrs. Harris is his son." We learned that a young man that answered his description, had been staying at the St. Charles hotel about the time of Mrs. Harris's disappearance, and he left about that time, and had not been seen since. So that confirmed Mr. Allwood in his suspicions.

The next day we started to his ranch on the east side of the Cascade mountains, about eighty miles from Jacksonville. We passed close by the lava beds, where years afterward, Captain Jack, of the Modock Indians, killed General Canby and Captain Thomas. It took us three days to journey to Allwood's ranch. The route was a rough one, and we had to travel slowly over the mountains. When we reached the ranch and had eaten our supper, we sat down to think over plans in reference to to our future case. Allwood said, "I think we had better keep close to the ranch several days and see if anything will turn up to enlighten us. During that time we can go up on the side of the mountain and kill a few grouse for a change of diet."

The next day we took our horses and rode along the foot of the mountains, when we saw a horseman riding towards us. We waited for him to come up. When he got near us, Allwood called out, "Hello, Joe, I am glad to see you. Where are you going?" "I am just looking around a little." "Well, Joe, let us go back to our ranch. I have something to say to you." Then we turned and rode back to the ranch, picketed out our horses, then went and sat down on the porch, and Allwood asked Joe if he had seen any one in the valley lately. "Yes, I saw three men riding in the valley ten miles above here. I watched them until they went up a dry ravine towards the mountains. I stayed there about two hours but saw nothing more of them." "How near were you to them, Joe?" "About two hundred yards." "Did they see you?" "No, I saw them coming about a mile away. I was upon the side of the mountain, and got behind some brush, and was watching them. After they started up the ravine, I saw them no more." "Joe, can you describe them?" "You bet I can! One was a tall young man, with dark hair, and dark complexion. Wore a brown hat with a broad brim. The other man I can't describe, but they looked as if they would cut a fellow's throat for fifty cents." Allwood turned and said, "They are the same men I saw when I was going down to Jacksonville." Joe was a half-breed Indian that lived at the Warm Springs agency in Oregon. Once or twice a

year he came out to Allwood's ranch and stayed a
month or two with him. He said, "Allwood is the
best fellow in the world. He saved my life one time
when I could not help myself. Now, I will be his
friend as long as I live." After supper I got a chance
to speak to Allwood, and asked if he could trust the
Indian with our secret. "Yes," he said, "he will be a
great help to us. He is sharp, and will do anything I
ask him to do for us, and a braver man never lived than
Joe." "Do you think he would be a good man to spy
out their stronghold?" "I don't think we could find a
better, and he will do anything we ask of him." "Well,
you talk to him, and I will take a stroll out among the
horses." When I returned they were still talking. I was
passing them when they called me to come and sit down.
Mr. Allwood said, "Joe has the same opinion of those men
that we have, and thinks he knows about where their
stronghold is located. Joe has promised me he will start
tomorrow and take about three day's provisions with him,
and if he finds where they are located, he will watch
and see if he can tell how many men there are, and if
there are any women." Look sharp to yourself, Joe,
and don't let them find you napping." Joe laughed.
"Well, Joe, find out as much as you can and return as soon
as possible, for we shall feel uneasy about you until
we see you coming back." Late in the evening of the
third day, Joe got back, tired and worn out, for he had not
slept but about two hours since he left us. We got
him something to eat, and told him to lay down and get
some rest before he told us anything about his trip.

He was soon fast asleep and never woke up until we called him for breakfast next morning. After he had eaten a hearty breakfast, he told his story.

CHAPTER XVI.

"When I left here I went straight to where I saw them ride up the gulch, to see if they had come out again. I found no track, except the one going up the gulch, so I knew it would not do for me to follow directly on the trail. I took up the side of the mountain, and followed near the gulch for five miles, then I heard horses' feet coming up the gulch, and dodged behind some rocks and waited to see who was coming. In a few moments I saw five men coming around the bend in the gulch, with three pack horses heavily laden. After they passed me, I followed along in sight of them, but kept back on the mountains. They traveled up the gulch about three miles, then took across the mountains and came within fifty yards of where I was concealed. They traveled about four miles over the mountains, then turned to the right and traveled about two miles, which brought them to a beautiful little cave, where there was a little spring with quite a stream of water flowing from it. There was quite a patch of timber back of the spring and grass in front of it. They rode straight to the timber, and I watched to see if they would come out. About thirty minutes later I saw two of them coming out with their horses, which they led down to the spring to drink. I stayed there till dark. By this time I was very thirsty, and crawled down to the spring to get a drink. While drinking, I heard some one coming down the path. I got behind a rock and crouched down. A man came to the spring with a bucket, and filling it, returned to the timber. I had noticed before dark, that on the left side of the timber, the mountain looked rough and craggy, so I thought the best thing I could do was to go around and find a good place to hide that I might watch and see what they were doing there. I was sure I was near their rendezvous and I was determined to find out where it was before I left. I saw nothing more of them during the night.

The night was very still; not a sound was to be heard except the howl of the mountain wolf at intervals. I could see the spring from my position, and a little after daylight I saw an old woman go to the spring with a bucket on her arm and a shawl thrown over her head. She filled her bucket and started back, not to the timber but to the west side of the mountain and vanished out of sight. Then I knew that there was their hiding place. I saw eight or ten men during the day, but none of them left. I saw several come from the mountain where the old woman disappeared. Late in the evening I saw the young man come out and sit down on a rock for a long time, his head resting on his hands and he seemed to be in a deep study. At last he got up and went back very slowly until he disappeared from my sight. That night there were two new arrivals and after that all was quiet during the night.   Early in the morning there was quite a stir in the camp.   About nine o'clock eight men rode out from the timber, only two going in the same direction across the mountain.   I thought if they did not get back that night I would have a chance to visit their camp and learn all I could about them.

Late in the evening I saw an old woman come out on the mountain leading a young woman, small in size. They sat down on a rock and entered into a spirited conversation, as I could tell by the young woman's wild gestures.   They sat there for some time, then slowly retraced their steps and were suddenly lost to sight.

The sun began to sink behind the mountain and the stars began to appear in the heavens above.   The robbers had left only one man to guard the place, and he was stationed on a point of the mountain just below the spring from where he could see the country for miles and miles away.   As soon as the shades of night o'erspread the little valley below, I took off my shoes and put on my moccasins and started on my perilous journey to examine the place where I saw them disappear.   I got down from my hiding place and crept cautiously along the mountain side until I came to the place I had seen the women last, then I stopped and listened and looked carefully around me.   I knew they must live in a cave and I thought I was very near to it.

I listened there for some time, then I heard a slight noise about fifty yards from me toward the foot of the mountain.   I could see a large rock in the direction of the sound and I thought the entrance to their hiding place

was behind the rock. I lay there on the ground for
some time, then crawled around to the rock and listened
but no sound could I hear. Then I crawled around until
I could see behind the rock and there, not ten feet from
where I lay, was a small opening that led back into the
cave. I crept up to the opening and looked in and about
twenty feet back I could see a light near the ground and
I supposed it came from under the door, so I crept in
and found it was a door. I listened there a few moments
and then crept back. Just as I had got back to the
mouth of the cave I heard someone coming not fifty feet
away. I lay flat on the ground and crawled along the
side of the mountain and had got about twenty feet away
when a man came to the mouth of the cave and gave a
signal which was answered from within. In a few
moments an old woman came to the door and said: "Is
that you, Bob?" "Yes," he growled out. Then she came
to the mouth of the cave and said: "What do you want?"
"I want to talk to the woman awhile. How does she
feel? Is she as sullen as ever?" "No, Bob, she is almost
dead with grief. I had a long talk with her this evening
and tried to get her to marry you but she said she would
rather die than be your wife. My dear son I think you
made a mistake when you brought her here, and I wouldn't
be surprised if it leads to something bad before it ends."
"Hold your tongue; I will hear no more of your nonsense.
I am bound to see her. I know she is as stubborn as a
mule, but I will bring her around before another week."
"Oh my son, listen! It may be the last time I will ever
appeal to you. I was once as innocent as that young

woman, but what am I now?—an outcast from society, hunted by the officers of the law, when once I was as innocent as the driven snow. Oh, my son, it was the love I had for your father that has brought me down to the lowest depths of despair. Son, for my sake spare that poor young woman! Take or send her back to her people." "Pshaw, old woman, that will never do; do you think I am such a fool as that. Take her back and get my neck stretched for the trouble? No! she shall be my mistress in spite of you and all the devils in the mountains."

The old woman sat still for some time before she spoke. Then she said, "You refuse my request? You know I have tried for years to get you to quit this wild life you are living, and have often warned you that the time would come when you'd wish you had taken mother's advice. I have been uneasy ever since this woman has been amoɪg us. I dreamed the other night that a band of soldiers attacked us, and killed or captured all of us, and took you prisoner." "You're an old fool. You are always prophesying something bad happening to my men." Then he turned and walked away in silence, and I came on back here."

After the half-breed had told all he had seen and heard, I told Mr. Allwood that something must be done, and that quickly, before that villain puts his threats concerning Mrs. Harris into execution. "Have you any plan for her rescue?" "There is only one way that I can see, and that is to send Joe to Jacksonville with a letter to the sheriff, explaining Mrs. Harris's danger, and ask him to come as quick as possible with about twenty men to my ranch. Joe can pilot them through the mountains to the back of my place, where they can hide their horses from any one traveling through the valley." We knew it would be too dangerous for us to try to rescue Mrs. Harris without help. So we wrote the letter and started Joe with it to Jacksonville, that very evening, with instructions to get back as soon as possible, and to cross the mountains after night, that they might run less risk of being seen. Allwood cooked something to eat for Joe to take along with him, and after we had eaten a hearty supper, and the sun had gone down behind the mountains, Joe started on his long journey. The next morning about ten o'clock we went up on the mountain and stayed there until late in the evening, watching to see if anyone was passing through the valley. We saw no one that day. We killed two grouse during the day, which we took home with us, and cooked for our supper. The next day Allwood said we would take our horses and ride up the valley about eight miles, to where a small stream came out of the mountains, about two miles from where Joe saw the bandits. Towards the head of the stream was a thick pine grove, where the deer would go and lie during the heat of the day. Just before we got to the grove, Allwood stopped, and went upon a high point to look over the valley and see if anybody was in sight. While standing there, he cast his eyes along the foot of the mountain, and saw four men riding over a ridge, about two miles

9 .

off, in the direction of the robber's cave, then we returned
to our cabin.

After we had eaten supper we sat and talked till
late in the night, then went to bed, hoping the sheriff
and his men would soon come. But the thought of the
coming conflict with the band of desperate men was
not pleasant to contemplate, and it drove the sleep from
our eyes, for we feared that some of us would never return
to our loved ones again, and it was as liable to be the one
as the other. When we rose from our beds the next
morning, the sun was just coming up. How beautiful
it looked, that calm, still morning. What a contrast to
the wild beating of our hearts, for we knew not what
the day would bring us. So it is with all mankind ; two-
thirds of all the trouble we have in this life is borrowed
from tomorrow. So it was with us; the day passed
quietly by, and Joe did not return till the fourth night
about ten o'clock. He brought the sheriff and ten men,
and had left them in the grove back of Mr. Allwood's
place, at the foot of the mountain. We told Joe to lay
down and take a nap, and we would get up and prepare
breakfast. While Allwood prepared breakfast, I went
out to where the men were and brought them to the house.
We soon had breakfast ready, and after we had eaten, we
fixed places for the men to lie down and take a much
needed rest, for they had not slept any since the night
before. In a short time all were fast asleep, and we let
them sleep until two o'clock in the afternoon ; we had
dinner ready for them, and after the meal was over,
Mr. Allwood and I took the sheriff aside and talked over

our plans for attacking the robbers. It was some time before we had our plans fully arranged. I suggested that it would be a good plan to send out two spies to examine the place and find out the number of men, and where their guards were stationed. It was agreed that Joe and Allwood should go, and as soon as the shades of evening had spread a mantle over the valley, they started, and about four o'clock in the morning they returned. They had seen five or six men sitting around their fire in the grove, about one hundred yards from the spring. Allwood said he crawled up near enough to hear part of their conversation. They were talking about a raid they had made on a settler's store over on the Klamath river, where one of their men got killed. "From what I could learn from their talk, there must be about eight or ten men at the grove now. There were two men on guard. We could see them, for the stars were shining brightly. They are placed about three hundred yards apart, and I think we can capture them without disturbing the men at the grove.

The sheriff said: "It will be almost impossible to take them alive, but if you can silence them without making too much noise do so." Then he called the men all together and said: "Gentlemen, the band of men we are going to attack are outlaws and murderers; if we can capture some of them alive, let us do so. Now men, you know your duty; be brave and all will be well. Mr. Allwood will take half of the men and go to the grove; I will take my men with Joe to lead us and go to where the other guard is stationed."

We waited until about ten o'clock that 'night and then mounting our horses we rode silently away.

It was about twelve miles to their rendezvous and we were to ride to within one mile of them and leave our horses in the care of a man and then on foot take the route that had been mapped out for us. After capturing the guards we were to crawl as close to their camp as possible, then lie low until the break of day would show us where the robbers lay; then at the crack of a rifle we were all to fire into them and then draw our revolvers and rush upon them. We got within two hundred yards of where the guard was sitting, when Allwood told us to stop and he would go and fix him. We sat down and waited anxiously for three quarters of an hour when Allwood returned and said he found him sitting on a big rock and thought he was asleep. He crawled up behind the rock then raised up and struck him with his gun on the back of his head. He fell from the rock without a groan and had hardly struck the ground when Allwood was on top of him. His head was split open. He lay there some time to see if his fall was heard by anyone but all was as still as death. Then Allwood got up and came back to us. It was now nearly four o'clock in the morning and we started very cautiously on our way to the little grove where the robbers lay asleep. When we entered the grove we saw a log cabin about two hundred yards in front of us; then we lay down and crawled up within about seventy-five yards of the cabin. We could see forms lying around on the ground in front of the cabin. We thought there must be eight or ten from the circle they formed. We lay there about two hours, when one of them got up and made a fire, lit his pipe and smoked awhile; then he spoke to the rest of the men telling them to get up. Daylight was fast making its appearance in the east and in about ten minutes he called to them again. They commenced getting up one at a time until six as rough looking men as ever I saw stood around the fire. Oh, how we longed to hear that rifle shot! We had to wait but a few minutes until the signal came. At the sound we jumped to our feet and fired five shots into them and the other boys did the same. We drew our revolvers and started in a run towards the cabin, and had got within fifty feet of the cabin when four men came out of the door with pistols in their hands and fired at us. We fired about the same time and the other boys came up behind them just at this time and also fired at them. Three of them fell and the other ran towards the cave, but Joe was too quick for him and caught him about fifty yards from the cave. Then followed a hard struggle. They dropped their pistols and drew their knives. He was a powerful man but Joe was more than a match for him. Some of the men ran to Joe's assistance and the sheriff called to Joe to spare the man's life and was soon there himself and slipped the handcuffs on. He placed three men at the mouth of the cave and took his prisoner back to the cabin. We found five of the men killed and four wounded and two of the wounded died that night. We had one man killed and four wounded. We dressed their wounds as well as we could.

The boys dug a long trench and laid the dead men in it and covered them up.

We learned from one of the men that was wounded that our prisoner's name was Bob, the Dare Devil. He was more dreaded than any man that lived in the western mountains and the leader of the worst band of cutthroats that ever lived on the Pacific coast. We tried to find out the number of men he had in his band, but he was sullen and we could get nothing from him. We left two men to guard the wounded prisoners and took Bob and went to the cave.

We asked him if there were any men in it, but he would not say a word. The sheriff put Bob in front and five of us entered the cave. About twenty feet back we found the door, which was locked. We knocked and a feeble voice within asked, "What do you want?" "Open the door, we are friends." We heard the key turn in the lock and the door flew open. To our surprise we found no one in the cave but the old woman and Mrs. Harris. The old woman was lying in a bed in a corner of the room. As soon as Mrs. Harris unlocked the door she turned and ran to the bed where the old woman was, for the first man that entered the door was the man who brought her there, and the very sight of him made her tremble. As soon as I entered she knew me and ran to me, crying: "Save me, save me! For God's sake don't let that man come near me!" "Don't be afraid Mrs. Harris," I said, "we are all your friends. Don't you see the handcuffs on that man? We have captured the entire band and have come to take you back to your friends." The old woman turned her head and looked at her son and with tears in her eyes she said: "Bob, I have been expecting this for years; may God have mercy on your soul." And with a wild despairing look in her eyes, sank back on her bed in a swoon. Mrs. Harris got some water and bathed her face for some time before she revived ; during that time Bob was taken back to the cabin where the other prisoners were.

As soon as the old woman came to herself and was able to talk, I asked her how many men there were in her son's band. " I don't think there are more than ten or twelve men." "How long has the band been living here?" "About four years," she said. 1 asked about her husband, and she said he was killed about six months ago in Oregon. Then she commenced crying again, and it was some time before she was quiet enough to talk. I asked where her son kept his stock. She said he kept it in a little valley about ten miles away, and she described the place to us. I asked if she knew the trail that led to the valley. She said, " You go down this little stream about one mile, then you will see a small cattle trail leading west. Follow that about ten miles, then turn to the north and follow that trail about one-half mile down a deep, craggy gulch which leads to the valley." " Thank you," I said, then turned to Mrs. Harris and asked her to go with me to Mr. Allwood's ranch. I told Mr. Allwood what the old woman said about the cattle, and that I would take Mrs. Harris back to his ranch for this was no place for her. I took her by the hand and led her out of the cave and down to the spring, where I left her a few moments to talk with Mr. Allwood. He said he would send some of the boys for the cattle, that they might be compelled, on account of the wounded, to remain there for a few days. As soon as the horses were brought up, I took Mrs. Harris back to the ranch. On the evening of the fifth day, Allwood, the sheriff and all the prisoners got back. Their wounds were doing fine, and he thought by riding slow they would be able to stand the trip. They had sent Joe and another man to hunt up the cattle. They found about one hundred·head of cattle and about fifty head of horses.

They left Joe and three other men to drive them over to Jacksonville. The next morning the prisoners were all right, and we all mounted our horses and rode away over the mountains.

They had found Mrs. Harris's horse and saddle and she had the satisfaction of riding her own horse back home again. It took us four days to get back to Jacksonville, for we had to ride slowly on account of the wounded prisoners. Soon after our arrival, we had them lodged safely in jail.

I took Mrs. Harris to her friend's house, Mrs. Waldon's. The great joy for them in this meeting, I will leave my reader to imagine.

In due time the prisoners were sentenced and sent to the penitentiary for life.

The night before the sheriff was to start with them, Bob got away, and has never been seen nor heard of since. The others are still in prison, if living.

In a few days Mr. Allwood started back to his lonely ranch in the mountains.   There is something about the wild and easy life of a man who lives in the mountains, that can not be found anywhere else.   I don't think J. ever saw a man who had lived long in the mountains, but wanted to go back there again.

I tried to get Mr. Allwood to go down to California with me, but he would not.   He said, "There is no place that seems like home to me except on the mountains, and I hope to be laid on the side of one when I die, where the wild birds can sing their plaintive songs over my grave, morning and evening, until the great day shall come when we all shall sing the same sweet songs as the birds now sing."

Dear friend, I don't think there is a place in the world where a man can have as grand conceptions of the Great Architect as he can while standing on some lone mountain top, looking at the little cascades pouring their waters over the craggy rocks here and there, thousands of feet above the sea level.   Then turn your eyes in another direction and see yon deep, craggy gulch thousands of feet below you, then turn your eyes up to the lofty peaks, as silent monuments to the Great Architect, for ages and ages gone by, and will continue to stand, no doubt, until time shall be no more.   So how can we blame him for wanting to go back to his mountain home ?

CHAPTER XVII.

I bade Mrs. Harris goodbye, and started for Sonoma county, California, in the Sacramento valley. I stayed there till February, 1870. Then I returned to old Missouri, and in the spring of 1878, I started down to New Mexico.

In due time, I landed in Las Vegas, which was the terminus of the Santa Fe railroad at the time, and it seemed to me that all the thieves and cut-throats in the country were located there.

The new town was built about one mile from the old Spanish town of Las Vegas. Midway between the two towns was a small creek, which was crossed by a bridge, and scarcely a night passed but some one was held up and robbed, at or near the bridge. I stayed there seven weeks, and during that time, there were four men killed. There were police in both towns, and although so many were robbed and murdered, they did not make a single arrest.

About three miles to the northwest, the hot springs are located. Thousands of invalids go there each year to bathe in its healing waters. It rests snugly at the foot of the mountains, and is a beautiful place to visit in summer.

I had to take a wagon from Las Vegas to Santa Fe. We started one afternoon, and the next night camped on the Pecos river, near the old Pecos church, which stands there as a monument to a race of people that has long since passed away. Who they were and where they came from is a mystery that will never be solved. The church has stood there for ages, defying the storms of the elements, but it is slowly crumbling away, and will soon be a thing of the past, like the tribe that built it.

The next day we traveled through the Apache Pass and camped on a little stream that flows through the mountains at a point where during the Mexican war many a soldier lost his life at the hands of the Indians.

There was no place for fifty miles that a wagon could be taken through this canon. The Mexicans called it the bloody pass. Before the railroad was built the merchants of Santa Fe got all their goods from some point on the Missouri river and they had to be hauled through this pass. Many wagon trains have been attacked here and the Mexicans who were with the trains were killed and their goods taken away by the Indians.

Before Kit Carson married an Apache squaw he had a hard fight here with the Indians. He had six men with him and they had gone about half way through the canon when the Indians attacked them in front and killed one of his men. The rest put spurs to their horses and dashed through the company of Indians, killing several as they went.

Late in the evening of the next day we arrived at Santa Fe. It was an old Indian town when the Knights of Horado took it from the Indians about three hundred and seventy-five years ago. Some of the adobe houses that the Indians built are standing there to this day.

Santa Fe is located at the foot of a spur of the Rocky mountains, seven thousand feet above the sea level. On a little flat on the mountain side about a half mile to the northeast, Gen. Kearney planted his cannon, threw up breastworks, raised the stars and stripes and commanded the town to surrender. His fort was about four hundred feet higher than the town. The citizens of the town raised a flag pole there and every Fourth of July the stars and stripes float proudly from its top.

It is a gradual descent from here to the Rio Grande, where the Pueblo Indians have their town which they call San Domingo. Their houses are all built of adobe and the entrance to them is from the top. The Indians built this way for protection against the wild tribes which made raids up and down the river and carried off many of their women and children.

I went from here to the Tahama Hot Springs sixty-five miles west.

While traveling over the mountains I saw in several places lava which had been thrown over the hills from the volcanoes. I could have picked up a peck of the stones called smoky topaz.

The second day about noon I arrived at the mouth of the Tahama creek, which is about ten miles from the Springs. All along the road and scattered over the valley could be seen pieces of old Indian pottery, ranging from the size of a dime to the size of a man's hand, and all having blue and black stripes running across them. For a distance of over twenty miles one could see the ruins of thousands of stone buildings scattered over the valley and on the Mesas on the mountain side, from one hundred to one thousand feet above the valley.

The Tahama Hot Springs are known all over the country for their healing properties. There are four springs situated on about one acre of land, three hot and one cold—one sulphur, one soda and one iron. While I was there I saw several brought there who had not taken a step for over a year, and by bathing in the waters for six weeks, they could walk without the aid even of a cane.

On the creek one mile above the springs the ruins of an old church are standing. The walls, standing about thirty feet apart, were fifty or sixty feet long, from six to nine feet high, six feet thick and were built out of flat stones. The people who built this place of worship have long since passed away. If I were to say it was built by the tribe of Ephriam, who could disprove it?

While at the springs I became acquainted with a Mexican who had a ranch on the Little Colorado river, about a hundred miles away. While talking to him one day he told me that several years before he had seen small specks of gold on a bar of the river about forty miles above his ranch, and if I would go with him we would prospect it. I told him I would go. He said he had a spring wagon and a good team and we could make the trip in three days. We had everything ready in two days and on the third day we started for the ranch. It was a rough road to travel with a team.

After a hard day's journey over a spur of the mountain we came in the evening of the second day to a beautiful grove of fir timber that grew on the bank of a little stream running close to the foot of the mountain. Here we encamped for the night. After we had eaten our supper and lighted our pipes we spread our blankets on the ground and sat down.

Gonsilas then told me that this beautiful grove was once haunted by a wild man and was shunned by both whites and Indians. The supposition was that the man seen in the grove was a celebrated duelist, who had killed several men in Old Mexico and whom the officers run out of the country. He also said that about six years ago a young hunter came into the valley to trap beaver. He had been told about the wild man in the grove, but his reply was: "I would like to see him." After he had been there about two weeks he took his gun early one morning and started to examine the grove. He had gone about half way through it when he came to a log and he sat down on it to rest. He had been sitting there but a short time when he saw a man coming towards him with a gun on his shoulder. He waited and the man came up and asked him what he was doing and if he wasn't afraid to travel through the grove alone for he might meet that duelist. The young man answered: "No, I'm not afraid to meet him." "What would you say if you happened to meet him?" "I would ask him to step off twenty paces and I would exchange shots with him." "What would you do if he was standing before you now?" "I would ask him to exchange shots with me."

"Well! young man, he stands before you, and I see you have a gun, so let's go and step off the ground."

"Oh, no! You can't be the man, for he would have shot me at first sight."

"No, young man, I never take the advantage of a man ; so come along, I will give you a fair show. You told me what you would do, so you have *got to do it.*" "You're a stranger to me, and I have nothing against you, so let us part in peace." "You made your brag what you would do, so shoulder your gun and come along."

Trembling all over the young man picked up his gun and followed the stranger to a cleared piece of ground. They walked to the center of it, then stopped facing each other. The young man said, "Give me a little time to write a few lines to my mother." After doing so he handed it to the man and said : "If I fall by your hand send this to my mother." He grasped the young man by the hand and said : "If I should fall let my body lay where it fell, and let the wild wolves tear the flesh from my bones and the birds of prey pluck my eyes from their sockets, and let my bones bleach in the sun, but tell no man where I fell." Then they turned their backs together, each stepped off twenty paces, turned and fired. At the crack of their guns the old man fell forward on the ground. The young man ran up quickly and spoke to him, but he was dead. He was left where he fell. The young man hunted and trapped for about two months, then disappeared. No one knew who he was nor where he went.

CHAPTER XVIII.

The next day we arrived at Mr. Gonsilas' ranch, and he introduced me to his wife and daughter, who bade me welcome to their home. The next day he took me over his ranch. He had one of the best stock and cattle ranches I ever saw, and he had it well stocked. He cultivated only about twenty acres, which was in the river bottom where he could irrigate it, for nothing was raised without irrigation. After we came back and had supper, he set chairs out on the porch, and we sat down for a social evening. I asked him how long he had lived here. He said all his life, that he was born on this ranch, and his father before him. He said, "My grand-father married a Mexican woman against the wishes of his wife's people, and they came out here and settled. They had been here but two years, when my father was born. About two miles above here at the big bend of the river, where my brother-in-law lives, is the house in which my father was born.

There is a sad story connected with that old house. My grandfather had five children—my father was the oldest. He was about twelve years of age when the Zuna Indians attacked their house. My grandfather had three Mexican men and four peons working for him. They had just finished breakfast one morning, when grandfather went to the door and saw twenty Indians crawling up to the house only about one hundred yards away. When they saw him at the door they jumped to their feet with a yell, and ran toward him. He had just time to shut and bar the door when the Indians struck the house with a wild and piercing war whoop. There were two windows in the house about five feet from the ground. The family got their guns and were ready for the first sight of an Indian. The Indians stood around the house for some time talking, then all were still. Grandfather knew they were up to something, but could not tell what it was. He kept a good lookout to see what they were going to do. On looking out from the window they saw four Indians with a long pole coming up the hill, about a hundred yards away. Then he knew they were going to try to break down the door, but it was made of thick slabs, and so well barred that he had no fear of them getting in through the door. They tried for some time to effect an entrance this way, but failed and gave it up. About the middle of the afternoon four or five Indians went up on the top of the house, and commenced to dig a hole in the dirt roof. The house was built of adobe, and the roof was covered with about two feet of dirt. It was not long until the Indians had dug down to the straw and brush that had been put on top of the logs that lay across the walls of the house. They had removed the straw and some of the brush, when they stooped down and looked into the room, and as they did so grandfather fired and shot one of them in the head, and he fell back with a groan. The

10

other Indians that were upon the roof yelled like wild demons. The sun had set behind the western mountains, when the Indians crawled off the roof, and they could hear them around the house till long after dark, then suddenly everything became as still as death. They did not know how soon the Indians might appear again, so kept a close watch all through the night. Early in the morning they found that all the water in the house was gone, and as soon as it became light enough for one to see any distance, grandfather said he would take the bucket and go down to the spring, which was about two hundred yards from the house, flowing out from under a big rock at the foot of the mountain.

He took his bucket and gun and started. As he stepped out of the house he looked in every direction but could see no signs of the Indians. He hurried down and had filled his bucket and had turned his face towards the house, when, "My God!" he cried, "just look there!" Within fifty steps of the house he saw twenty Indians running to the door that was standing open. He dropped his bucket and fired and one of the Indians fell dead on the doorstep. He loaded his gun as quickly as he could and started towards the house on the run. He had gone but a short distance when they saw him. With a wild yell they made for him. He fired and again brought down an Indian; the others jumped behind some rocks lying in the yard and began firing back at him. About this time two more Indians came out of the house and as they stepped out grandfather shot one of them. With another yell they again started for him and he ran for his life.   He knew of a deep gulch where a little stream came running down from the mountain and if he could only reach that before the Indians overtook him he would have some chance for his life.   He was swift on foot and while running the first mile he was far enough ahead to stop and load his gun, but by the time he did that two Indians had come within seventy-five yards of him.   He raised his gun and fired and the front Indian fell; the other stopped until the rest came up.   He loaded his gun again and ran on towards the gulch, the Indians all after him, but he was soon out of their sight; then he went on somewhat slower until he reached the gulch, where he waited to see if the Indians were still following him, but after waiting some time he went on up the gulch.   The farther up he went the more craggy and wild it appeared.   He soon heard the falling of water and saw where the little stream in the gulch was pouring its waters over the craggy rocks, and falling about ten feet where it dashed itself into foam on the rocks below.

About fifty yards below the little fall there were two rocks which stood out from the mountain about twenty feet from the bottom of the stream.   These rocks were about two feet apart.   By going in between these rocks and turning a little to the right you could see a small entrance, and by going in for about ten feet you came to a good sized room.   Here he entered and stayed till night had spread its mantle over the valley.

Then he started back to his ranch and when he got in sight of the house he saw that it was still standing.   He crept up to the open door and listened.   All was still as the grave. He went in, struck a light, and "Oh, my God, look there!" he cried, for on the floor before him lay his wife and three children scalped. He fell on his knees beside them and wept bitter tears of sorrow at their untimely end. There on his knees by the side of his murdered wife he made a solemn vow to never rest until he had avenged the death of his loved ones. In the next room lying on the floor he found his three Mexican men dead also. He looked around for his son and daughter who were nowhere to be seen and then he knew that the Indians had taken them prisoners and carried them off to their stronghold in the Black forest.

"Oh, my God!" he cried, "what have I done that my loved ones should be killed and cut up like wild beasts!" He walked around the house like a man who had lost his reason. For hours he kept up this silent tread. Not a sound was heard in this once happy home except the wild beating of his own heart. At last he stopped, took a last long look at his dead and walked out of the house. He got a spade, dug a grave and laid his wife and children in it together and covered them up. Then he knelt down upon the grave and with a sad wail, cried: "Sleep on dear wife; no sound of the war-whoop will ever wake you again." He then went back to the house, got the Mexicans and buried them.

The Indians had carried off everything in the house that was of use to them. , There was a trap door in the kitchen that led to the cellar. This the Indians had not found. There were two or three hundred pounds of flour and quite a lot of sugar and coffee here. He got his horses and carried this to the cave in the mountain, for he said he could never again live in the house until he had avenged the death of his loved ones. So he took everything he had up to the cave in the mountain.

My grandfather happened to find this cave several years before the Indians attacked his house. There was an old man who had been seen in the valley for several years. No one knew who he was or where he lived. One day grandfather was riding over his ranch, and as he came back to the mouth of the gulch, he saw the old man going up the gulch. He got off the horse and followed to see where he went. About three miles up the gulch he entered the cave, then grandfather turned and went back home. The old man generally went through the. valley about once every week. Months passed and the old man made his regular trips, but at last they stopped. He had not been seen for over four weeks when grandfather went up to see what had become of him. He found the cave without any trouble, and entering found the old man dead in one corner, lying on his blankets. By the looks of his long white beard and hair, he must have been upwards of eighty years. The next morning grandfather took a spade and buried the old man in a grove of pine trees about fifty yards below the cave and piled some rocks upon the grave to mark it. After grandfather got all his things into this cave, he sat down to rest, for it was late in the evening. He had sat there but a short time when he heard a noise. He crept to the mouth of the cave and listened, looking closely in every direction. On the other side of the gulch about two hundred yards away he saw an Indian creeping along the mountain side. He stepped back, got his gun and came to watch the Indian, to see what he was up to. He came down the side of the mountain within about fifty yards of where grandfather was, and stopped to look around, when grandfather shot him. He tumbled down the side of the mountain and fell in the gulch below. Early in the morning grandfather went down to see what had become of his Indian. When he got down to where he lay, to his surprise, he found that instead of an Indian, it was a Mexican he had killed. After examining him he recognized him as being the worst man in that part of the country. He had been living with the Indians for several years, making raids on the defenseless settlers, killing men, women and children, and driving off their stock. So upon making this discovery, grandfather felt very proud that he had killed the desperado. Every day grandfather would take a stroll down the side of the mountain to the valley to look for fresh signs of the Indians who might be passing through there. One day while looking he saw where three or four Indians had passed that morning. So he followed their tracks up the valley for about two miles to where a spur of the mountain came down close to the river. He saw that the Indians would have to cross this rock point as they came back, or cross the river a mile below. He hunted around and soon found a good place to hide, then lay down to wait for them. Late in the evening, he saw three Indians coming slowly up the valley. He waited until they came almost abreast of him, then fired, and killed the foremost one. The others jumped behind some rocks. Grandfather loaded his gun as quickly as he could and kept a close lookout to see where they had gone. He had lain there but a short time when he raised up, and saw them about thirty feet away on the other side of the ridge. They saw him at the same time and they both fired. One of the Indians gave a wild yell and fell dead. Grandfather started for the other and struck at him with his gun, but the Indian warded off the blow, then they came together, clinched, and both fell to the ground. They rolled over and over, first one on top, then the other. They had rolled about thirty feet when grandfather's head struck a rock, and he had to release his hold on the Indian. The Indian was on top in a moment, and raising his knife, gave a a wild exultant yell preparatory to plunging it in grandfather's breast, but before the yell had left the Indian's mouth a ball came crashing through his skull. A Mexican ran up and pulled the dead Indian off and helped grandfather to his feet, but he was so stunned by the blow on his head that it was some time before he could stand alone. When he could, and saw who it was that had saved his life, he threw his arms around the man and cried, "God bless you, my true and noble friend! How came you here in time to save my life?" "I was coming up the valley and when near the mouth of the gulch I heard a gun fired up this way, so I started up here to see about it. When I turned the point of the hill about a hundred yards back, I saw two Indians crawling up the hill. I was watching them, when I saw you raise up and fire. Then I broke into a run, and as you and the Indian were rolling down the hill, I stopped, and had my gun ready to fire the minute I got a chance. When he raised his knife I shot, and none too soon, for in another second the knife would have been buried up to the hilt in your heart." Pedro was the name of the Mexican who saved grandfather's life. As soon as he was able to travel, Pedro took him home. That night he told Pedro the sad story of the Indians killing all of his family except the oldest boy and girl, whom they took as prisoners. Pedro lived in a little town fifty miles down the river, and he thought that if they were to go back there they might raise a company to go with them and rescue the children from the cruel Indians. It was late in November when they arrived at the town. It was impossible to raise a company large enough to attack the Indians in their stronghold at that time of the year with any degree of success.

CHAPTER XIX.

They said that if he would wait until spring they would do everything in their power to raise a company large enough to wipe out the Indians at one blow. So he gave up all hopes of rescuing his children that winter.

He got Pedro to go back with him, and with a sad heart he left the town. That winter, while hunting in the mountains, they both had many narrow escapes from the Indians.

Spring had come and the cold winds of the north had ceased to blow, and, instead, the soft breezes of spring could be felt as they blew up the valley and played among the branches of the trees that grew on the mountain side.

About this time grandfather and Pedro were out near their house one day, when they saw a man riding up the valley towards them. He came up and asked where Mr. Gonsilas lived. Grandfather told him that was his name. Then the man said he had been sent up there by the captain of volunteers to tell him that they had a company of one hundred men and were waiting for two more companies of volunteers that were coming up from near the border of Old Mexico to join them, and that they would all be at the ranch in eight or ten days at the most. The time soon passed, and the little army arrived at grandfather's and camped near the spring. The company was commanded by an old Indian fighter named Juan Valego. They stayed at the spring two days and sent out their spies to find the best place to cross the mountains. It was fifty miles to the Indian town which was built at the edge of the Black Forest in a cave at the foot of the mountains. It took them three days to reach the north end of the forest, and the town was built at the south end. It was late in the evening when they reached the forest which was about two miles long. They found a beautiful little stream running down through the mountains, and there they camped for the night.

The captain sent out spies to see and examine the town and find the best place to attack it. They were gone about four hours and on their return, they brought with them a young Indian about fifteen years old whom they had captured while coming back. They reported that they had gone about two-thirds of the way around the town which was standing in a hollow cave right back against the mountain, and it seemed that the rock stood almost perpendicular, from twenty to fifty feet high for about two-thirds of the distance around the town. By keeping close up to the side of the grove it would bring you out at the main entrance on the east side of their stronghold. They saw but two Indian sentinels on guard. The young Indian they had captured was going towards the town, and lying in wait for him, they jumped and caught him before he saw them, telling him that if he made the least noise they would cut his throat. They bound his hands together and brought him to camp.

Nearly all the Indians in the country could understand some of the Mexican language, so they asked him how many warriors there were in the town. "I don't know." "Have any left town lately?" "Yes." "How many?" He held up his hands five times, (that meant fifty.) "Have they any prisoners?" "Yes." "How many?" He held up his hands twice. They asked if the Indians kept them confined. He answered "Yes." Then they asked him in what part of the town they kept them confined. He answered, "Close by the mountain." When they were through talking with him they put a guard over him. Then the captain called the different officers of the command and told them of the young Indian's conversation. The colonel told the men to get ready for the fight, and they would begin their march at three o'clock. Then he called the two spies, and told them to start at two o'clock and to quiet the two guards that stood at the gap leading to the town without making any noise if possible.

In a short time they were on their way to the Indian town. The two spies were there waiting for them and not a sound could be heard except an occasional bark from an Indian dog.

The colonel divided his men into two companies and started up through the town, and had gone but a short distance when all the dogs in the different parts of the town began barking and in a few minutes the Indians came out to see what the racket was. When they saw the enemy they ran yelling in every direction. This brought a hundred men, women and children out into the street and the settlers began firing at them. They ran up the street towards a big adobe house where there were about twenty warriors, who made a hard fight for about thirty minutes, when they were routed after killing three of the men and wounding several. They then ran to a large house in which the chief of the tribe lived. The house, which was built of stone, stood with its back against the bluff, with a stone wall about six feet high surrounding it. About all the warriors of the village had collected here by this time.

There was no way to attack this place except from the front, for the back stood against the bluff where it was solid rock from fifty to one hundred feet high. There was but one opening in the wall and that was a small gate in front of the house. They knew it would not do to try to get through the wall here because the Indians would kill half the soldiers before they got through the gate. The wall ran north and south. The colonel divided his men into two squads, the one going north and the other south.

They had marched about one hundred yards each way from the house, when they ran for the wall; then took along the wall until they made a solid line all around. Then the colonel had one of the soldiers to go back and look for the other company and tell them that they were against the wall out of reach of the Indians' guns and for them to go around on the mountain to the back of the house and fire into the Indians and draw them to the back of the house. While the Indians were looking the other way they could climb the wall and attack the Indians with their sabers. In about an hour firing commenced on the top of the cliff. The soldiers then scaled the wall and a bloody hand-to-hand fight ensued. The soldiers used sabers and the Indians used knives. The soldiers killed or wounded all the Indians excep·ing the old chief, who was a very powerful man, and killed every man who came within reach of his arm. He jumped through a window and escaped. What a sight when the fight was over! The floor covered with blood and here and there a soldier and a warrior lying side by side with the life blood slowly ebbing away. The cries of the wounded and dying were heart rending. As soon as the soldiers on the mountain saw the rest scale the wall they ran down the mountain side to the village and set fire to it. Ten of the boys were left to guard the house, while the sergeants were dressing the soldiers' wounds, and the rest went in search of the prisoners whom they soon found.

There were about twenty of them guarded by a few old squaws. As soon as grandfather's children saw him they ran to him and fell on his neck, crying as though their little hearts would break. They took the children down to the gap where ten soldiers had been left on guard. Grandfather was left there with the children, and the rest went back to the village to burn everything that could be burned.

Some were to bring the wounded men to the gap, and

some way was to be arranged to carry them back to the camp. There were thirteen killed and eighteen wounded, four of them so badly wounded that they had to be carried on stretchers. While some were making stretchers, the rest buried the dead at the south end of the grove.

They camped at the gap that night, and early the next morning they went back to their old camp on the little stream at the north end of the Black forest.

On the evening of the second day one of the spies brought news that about fifty warriors were coming up the creek about six miles below camp. At that point there was a very narrow pass in the mountains through which the Indians would have to pass. If they could reach it first they could surprise the Indians so completely that nearly all could be killed before they could get away. In a few minutes seventy-five men were on the road to the pass. They had just formed in line along the side of the pass when they saw the Indians coming. They waited until the Indians were in the pass then fired at them from both sides of the pass. More than half of the Indians fell at the first fire. They were taken so completely by surprise, that those who escaped the first volley wheeled their horses and started down the canon as fast as they could go without firing a single shot. There were but few Indians who escaped.

The soldiers got back to camp about eleven o'clock, and were so rejoiced at their victory that it was long past midnight when they fell asleep.

The company had to stay there four days before the wounded were able to be moved. During this time they examined the Black forest. This strip of land was so densely covered with pine and fir trees that in mid-day it was almost dark. About a quarter of a mile from the village, there was a cleared space with a solitary fir tree in the center. Around it were ashes, the remains, no doubt of many fires, and on the tree were marks made by cords which had held many prisoners while they were slowly burned to death.

On the morning of the fifth day the wounded were able to start back if they traveled slowly. By twelve o'clock they were all on the road, and in three days were at grandfather's ranch.

They stayed there ten days, and by that time the wounded were so much improved that they wanted to go on home. So they bade grandfather goodbye, and started back to the little town on the river fifty miles below. Grandfather persuaded Pedro to stay with him for he would be lonely with no one but his two little children. So he stayed and worked that summer.

That fall grandfather took my father and my aunt to Chihuahua, and put them in the Sisters' school to stay five years. He brought a Mexican man and his wife back with him to take care of his house and ranch while he was gone, for he intended to go down to Lower California to the old St. Gabriel Mission, where he had friends whom he had not seen for many years. He took Pedro with him.

CHAPTER XX.

And when he bade adieu to his old home, the tears ran down his cheeks like rain, for he was thinking of those loved ones sleeping in that lonely grave. "Sleep on," he cried, " I am going away but no mortal sound will ever wake you again."

The third day after leaving his ranch they stopped for the night at a little stream where the Oatman family had been massacred by the Navajo Indians fifty-six years before.

The next day, while passing over a spur of the mountains, they came in sight of the Death valley. About a mile from the valley they came to a spring which was flowing out from the rocks at the foot of the mountain. It was about four in the afternoon, so they camped for the night. They picketed their horses, for there was plenty of grass growing along the little stream. They filled their canteens and were ready for an early start the next morning. After eating supper they lay down and slept soundly until next morning.

While grandfather built the fire Pedro went to look after the horses, but they were gone. He went to the place where he had driven the stake and saw where some one wearing moccasins had been walking, so he knew the Indians had stolen their horses.

Grandfather was about forty years old at this time, weighed about one hundred and ninety pounds, and was very stout and active. When Pedro came back and told him the Indians had taken their horses he said "The thieving rascals! But we'll get even with them yet." They were in a bad predicament, about two hundred miles from the nearest settlement. They ate breakfast and talked over what would be best for them to do, finally concluding to follow their trail, and get back their horses if possible.

They had food enough to last a week, and after packing it up, started on the trail which ran to the northwest, and was very plain, so they had no trouble in following it. In the middle of the afternoon, the trail turned west across the mountain. They followed it until night, then went into camp. The day had been very warm, and they had used nearly all the water in their canteens. They were very tired and hungry after their hard day's travel, so they ate a cold supper and lay down to sleep. The next morning they had started by daylight. About ten o'clock they reached the summit, and sat down to rest. What a beautiful sight. Not a tree or bush grew near the summit. At last Pedro said, "I think we will have a hard time catching those red devils." Grandfather answered that they would pay dearly for their theft when they were caught. They traveled all day, and went into camp that night where the Indians had camped the night before. The wind was disagreebly cool, for they were still near the summit. They looked around for some sheltering rock, but could see none,

11

therefore went on and found some rocks after going about a mile. After spreading their blankets and sitting down, Pedro said, "Have you any water in your canteen, for I am very dry and haven't a drop in mine?" "My God," said grandfather, "I don't know what we will do if we don't find water soon. I haven't more than a pint left. I hope tomorrow we will find plenty. The Indians surely would never have taken this route had they not known where there was plenty of water." The next morning found them upon the trail after eating some cold food. They traveled about five miles over lofty peaks and deep gulches, and finally the trail turned down the mountain. Pedro said he didn't see how he could stand it another day without water for he was then very dry. "Be of good cheer, my friend," said grandfather, "I think we will find water before the sun goes down." "God grant that we may," said Pedro.

They traveled down the mountain and were on the last hill when they sat down to rest. About a mile below, where the trail struck the valley, was a grove of trees. Close to the hill at the edge of the grove, they saw smoke ascending from a pile of charred sticks lying on the ground. They crawled back off the hill for they knew it was not safe there, and crawled closely along the foot of the mountain towards the place where they had seen the smoke.

They had got within two hundred yards of the fire, when they saw four Indians sitting around it. About fifty feet from them was a nice spring of water, and at the sight they felt almost wild, for they had not had water for two days.   After their hard journey over the mountains without water that length of time, then to come in sight of it, and find it guarded by deadly foes twice their number was enough to try the bravest heart.

The sun went down behind the western mountains and night was fast spreading its mantle over the little valley, when grandfather told Pedro that as soon as it got dark, and the Indians lay down, he would take his canteen and go to the spring.   They knew it would not do to try to get water sooner, so waited as patiently as possible although the minutes seemed like hours, and Pedro's tongue had swelled almost out of his mouth.   They waited four hours before the Indians wrapped their blankets around them and lay down for the night.   Grandfather waited half an hour longer, then started on his perilous journey for water.   He kept close to the mountain that he might be in the shadow.   Pedro waited what seemed to be hours before grandfather got back.   When he did he would not let Pedro have but little at a time, until his great thirst was satisfied.

They ate a little supper and got their guns in good trim, for they thought they could crawl down and each shoot one, and then knock the other two down as they jumped from their blankets.

They waited till midnight, then crept cautiously up to within ten steps of the Indians, then fired, each killing one.   The other Indians jumped up, and as they did so, grandfather and Pedro knocked them down with their guns, and took their knives and cut their throats.

They then examined the camp, and found their bridles

and saddles and half of a deer which was very welcome to them, as they were about out of grub.   They pulled the Indians out into the grove, then went back, built up the fire, and soon had their venison roasting. After eating a hearty meal they sat down to talk over their plans.   Grandfather said he doubted if the four Indians were all of the band.   That the rest might be out hunting and would be back the next day, and that they had better take all the ammunition they could find, and hide the guns, so if any more Indians came, they would think the others had gone on.   They took everything out of camp and went into the grove about two hundred yards and lay down.   It was not long until they were sound asleep, and the sun was shining brightly when they awoke.   They cautiously raised up and looked around them, but all was still.   Not a sound was heard but the songs of the birds in the trees overhead.

They ate a cold lunch, as they thought the smoke might betray them, filled their canteens, and were discussing whether they had better try to find their horses then or wait until noon, when Pedro said: "Listen!   Don't you hear that?"   They listened and heard something like a growl, and came to the conclusion that it was some wild beast which had found the bodies of the dead Indians. They kept quiet, for they didn't want to be found by the beast for fear they would have trouble in getting rid of it.   In a short time more came to join in the work of tearing the flesh from the Indians' bones.   Their growls could be heard for a mile.   Grandfather and Pedro climbed a tree and from there they could see the animals.

They were mountain lions, four in number. They kept up a terrible fight for twenty minutes, and almost killed one of their number. They hung around growling and snapping at each other for about two hours, then slowly went away. Pedro said, "That beats the devil! Don't you think so Gonsilas? I would give my horse and all I have if I was just back home." " Don't be discouraged," said grandfather, " we will come out all right."

They then got down and went to look for their horses, expecting to find them at the upper point of the grove, then to bring them back to the spring, water them, and pack up and leave the place. They found them in a grassy flat above the grove. They soon had everything ready, and after eating their dinner, they mounted and rode away. They traveled up the valley about twelve miles, then crossed to the foot of the mountain to the west, and traveled about a mile, when they reached a deep gulch, which they stopped to examine, and about two hundred yards up the gu'ch, they found a spring, and watered their horses and camped for the night.

Next morning they crossed the mountain and came to the big Colorado river, just above where the Santa Fe road crossed the river, and here they camped for the night. At four o'clock in the morning, they crossed the desert to the westward, a distance of seventy-five miles. It was ten o'clock at night when they came to a little stream that runs close to the foot of the San Bernardino mountains. They stayed there three days to let their horses recruit a little, and a three days' ride took them to St. Gabriel mission in Lower California. Grandfather found his old friend who was glad to see him.

At the end of five years grandfather came back by way of Chihuahua, bringing my father and aunt back with him to his old home where my brother-in-law is now living. They had been living here two years when my father went back to Chihuahua and married and brought his wife home with him, and grandfather gave him the ranch I am living on. My aunt got acquainted with a young man while at school who lived in the town, and a few years after my father married, my aunt's acquaintance came out to make my father a visit. He fell in love with my aunt, and father and grandfather having no objection, they were married and lived with grandfather till he died. My aunt died soon after but my uncle lived to be quite old. They had no children and when my sister married she and her husband persuaded him to come and live with them. At his death he willed all his property to them."

I asked Mr. Gonsilas what had become of his father and he said he was killed. "He had started to take a drove of sheep down to Chihuahua, the closest market, and gone a little more than half way when the Indians made a raid on him, killing him and all his hands and driving off the sheep. We never got any of them back, neither did we ever hear of them again. The sad affair caused the death of my mother. She pined away and died within three months after she heard the sad news of her husband's untimely death."

The name of Mr. Gonsilas' brother-in-law was Frank Pachecco. We had been up to see him several times and told him we were going up the river to prospect for gold and persuaded him to go with us.

CHAPTER XXI.

Gonsilas said that if we found no gold we could have a good time hunting, as there was plenty of bear and deer in the mountains and we could spend a good week in that way and have a grand time.

In two days we were on the road, traveling about twenty miles the first day. We had brought some fish-hooks with us and that evening we caught some fine trout, enough for supper and breakfast.

The next day about the middle of the afternoon we reached the bar. We worked hard all day, tried several places but found nothing but a few specks of fine gold that would not pay us for our work.

We had been there two days when Mr. Pachecco said we had better try our luck hunting in the mountains; that he knew of a little stream on the other side that we could get to by the middle of the afternoon and at the head of the gulch was a fine place for deer. We packed up and started early the next morning and got there about three in the afternoon and went into camp.

That evening Pachecco said he would take his gun and go up the gulch to see if he could find any signs of deer. He had been gone about an hour when he returned with a fine doe on his shoulder. We had a nice mess of roast for supper and after eating we sat around talking over our plans. We were up and had breakfast before light the next morning and were ready to start up the mountain by daylight.

We went up to the head of several gulches we had seen coming over and killed five fine deer, and it was late before we got them to camp. The next day we concluded to jerk the meat, which we did by driving forked sticks into the ground and laying other sticks across them and putting the meat, which had been sliced, upon them. By evening it would all do to pack up and take home with us when we went.

About three o'clock in the afternoon Gonsilas took his gun and went up the gulch for a little hunt. He had been gone about one-half hour when we heard his gun and in a short time we thought we heard him halloo. We waited and listened a moment then we heard him again. We took our guns and started up to where he was and soon we heard him again. Then we knew something was wrong, so we hurried as fast as we could. We soon saw him; he was in the top of a little tree close to the edge of the gulch. At the foot of the tree we saw a huge cinnamon bear, which went off down the gulch as soon as it heard us coming. Then we laid down and laughed till the tears rolled down our cheeks to see Gonsilas up the tree, bareheaded, with his gun lying on the ground at the foot of the tree. He crawled down the tree and picked up his gun before he said one word. Then he said: "It must be d——d funny to you, but I don't see where the laugh comes in." Then we roared with laughter and asked him to tell us how he came to be up the tree. He said: "Do you think I am big enough fool to stay on the ground when a big bear is after me? I only beat her to the tree about ten steps. I was crossing that point there about fifty yards above when I heard a noise and looking around I saw two cubs down in the gulch; I fired at them and just as I did so I heard a noise, and looking in the direction from which it came, saw the old bear not more than fifty yards away coming at me with her mouth wide open. Then I took to the tree just in time to get out of her reach and began to halloo for help. I had almost come to the conclusion that you were not coming to help me." He then showed us where he had shot the cubs and killed one. Pachecco went down and brought it up and told Gonsilas to take it back to camp, which he did.

Pachecco and I then went in search of the old bear. We had gone about three hundred yards when we saw her and the other cub climbing up on the other side. I shot at her and broke her back and she fell over, rolling to the bottom of the gulch. Pachecco ran down close to where she was and she raised herself upon her fore legs and growled at him so loudly you could have heard her half a mile. He shot her in the head and also killed the cub. We skinned them and took their hides back to camp. That evening we got everything ready to start back to Gonsilas' ranch.

We started back the next day and reached Pachecco's a little after sundown. He wanted us to stay all night with him, but Gonsilas was anxious to get home, which was about three miles further on. That night I told Mrs. Gonsilas and her daughter how we found Gonsilas up a tree with his hat off, hallooing like a good fellow, and his gun lying at the foot of the tree. They laughed heartily at him, asking him how he felt while sitting up there, and if he was scared much. He said, "No. Not while I was in the tree, but before I got there my boots rattled."

We spent a very pleasant evening laughing and talking. The next morning I told Mr. Gonsilas I wanted to go back to Santa Fe, for I had been away longer than I had expected to be, and would like for him to take me to Coolidge. He told me to wait three or four days as he had some business to attend to, then he would take me. While he was gone, he left me with his wife and daughter, Dolendo.

Dolendo was about eighteen years old. Her form was perfect, with long black hair which hung below her waist. Her eyes were dark, and when she looked at you with her laughing eyes, you would say that she was one of the most lovely women you ever saw. So you cannot blame me for staying not only four days, but a week longer. Every day we took a ride over the valley, and sometimes went far up the mountain to look at the grand and noble works of the Creator, but when I turned my eyes to look at her face, I could not help feeling that there before me, stood one of the most perfect beings of all the Creator's handiwork.

I soon bade them goodbye, and Mr. Gonsilas and I started for Coolidge, where we arrived late in the evening. It was a small place where the railroad had just started a round house. There was one boarding house and one butcher shop. From seventy to one hundred men took their meals at the boarding shanty.

That evening I met an old acquaintance who was head carpenter on the road. I told him where I had been, and he persuaded me to stay and make some depot seats for him. While I was there, several men were held up and robbed.

The second day I was there, three men came to the station with Winchesters on their shoulders and big revolvers in their belts. They camped in a big shanty, about three hundred yards from the round house. These men were the robbers. They got so bold a man could hardly step out of the house after dark without being held up. Every night after they came, some one was robbed. They robbed the butcher while he was going from the telegraph office, not over two hundred yards from the station. And as the operator was going to supper they robbed him.

At this they sent for the sheriff twelve miles away. Just before daylight the sheriff and his deputies arrived. Getting about twenty more men, they surrounded the cabin, calling for the men to come out and surrender, but they received no reply. There was but one door and soon the men came out, revolvers in hand, and fired into the crowd, then ran. Every one who had a gun began shooting at them. One went about fifty yards then fell, the second one got about one hundred and fifty yards before he fell, and the last one got about four hundred yards.

That was one of the biggest excitements I ever saw, and I don't care to witness another such a one. Three of the sheriff's men were killed, and he was wounded and died about a week afterwards. After that fight, the station was very quiet while I was there. When I finished my work I returned to Santa Fe.

My story is finished, but I cannot lay down my pen without telling you of the sad fate of Miss Dolendo Gonsilas. Her mother wrote and told me of the sad fate that befell her only daughter.

"On last Sunday, the day being so nice and warm, Dolendo said she would ride out for a little while. So she took her book and went to the foot of the mountain and hitched her horse to a little bush, then climbed up the mountain to where there was a large rock lying on the edge of the cliff, where oft she had gone before, and read for hours and hours. We waited for her, this time, until it was almost dark, then her father took his horse and went to look for her. He soon found her horse tied at the foot of the mountain, and called and called for her, but no answer came. So he started to go around to the foot of the cliff, when oh, what a sight met his eyes. There on the rocks, at the foot of the cliff. lay our daughter, dead. She had fallen from the cliff above, for there on the rock her book was lying where she had been sitting."

She was the most beautiful woman I ever saw, too pure and innocent to live in this cold world, so the angels came, and took her to that beautiful paradise, beyond the Dark River of Death.

THE END.

www.ingramcontent.com/pod-product-compliance
Lightning Source LLC
Chambersburg PA
CBHW030905050726
47500CB00009B/1101